SISTER SIMON'S MURDER CASE

MARGARET ANN HUBBARD

Sister Simon's Murder Case

THE BRUCE PUBLISHING COMPANY • *Milwaukee*

F
H 86

Library of Congress Catalog Card Number: 59–10218

© 1959 Margaret Hubbard Priley
MADE IN THE UNITED STATES OF AMERICA

TO THE MAN IN MY LIFE WHO, THOUGH HE
SELDOM HAS TIME TO READ MY BOOKS, IS
NEVERTHELESS MY MOST DEVOTED FAN AND
PRESS AGENT, MY EVER LOVING HUSBAND, JOE

SISTER SIMON'S MURDER CASE

Chapter One

THE slim little woman sat on the green bench in front of the curio shop, her eyes shifting with the crowd that passed inches beyond her knees. Too bad she could not enjoy herself in this vacation mecca. But she tried at least to relax, every time she thought of it. At these times she would straighten her small shoulders, remember how her hair always straggled in the heat — for the August mugginess still hung over into the evening — and feel for wisps to tuck under. Then her hand would go a little higher to touch the three pink roses on the hat. The roses looked nice. She had snipped new edges on them and pressed the veil over wax paper. The cotton dress was too wide in the neck, but fastened up with the brooch, it was all right. Appearance was unimportant anyway. She had come here with a purpose. In a minute or two she would get up from the bench, go down the long cement stairs that led from Main Street to the little park on the water front. . . .

She couldn't help it, her chin trembled. Fingering her chin, she felt the tiny white whisker that persisted in growing in the mole. She should have thought to pull it out. But it was no wonder, really, that small things slipped her mind.

The Indian on the other end of the short bench began to

1

scratch, thoroughly. Under the bench his dog cuffed an ear, tapping the little lady's ankle. She moved her foot, then raised her small suitcase from the pavement and stood it between herself and the Indian. He went on scratching.

The little woman drew a long breath and set her gaze deliberately upon the crowd. All were vacationers, all in pursuit of amusement. That was why she felt so apart from them. But she liked the general bedlam — snatches of conversation, jukeboxes blasting from open shops, the solid zoom of traffic uphill from the river and the hooting of downbound cars for the right of way on the narrow turn to the bridge, the whistles of boats seemingly distant but actually right down behind the buildings, the roar of skates from the roller rink. And the evening had a frivolous smell of popcorn and arid summer and engine exhaust that called up pictures of travel and fun. A bus prowled past, nosing between automobiles. Its breath was different, heavy with burned kerosene. At every stop this afternoon the little woman had caught that oily stench and it had made her sick. The same nausea rolled over her now. Only, to be fair, she couldn't put all the blame on the bus. She always felt sick to her stomach when she was worried. And tonight she was not only worried, she was in actual physical dread.

Her hand flew again to her hat, a reflex so abrupt that her elbow knocked the suitcase against the Indian. He turned, mildly curious.

"Excuse me — so careless of me!" she murmured.

Jumping up, snatching the suitcase, she dived into the crowd. No more dallying. Get it over. Using the suitcase as a rudder, she pushed between a teen-age couple who were strolling arm in arm, shoved aside a middle-aged man who bristled, "Well, pardon me for living!" and ran hard into a small boy. The boy squealed in the manner of children who are much too tired and use any excuse to raise a commotion. His mother, a fat,

moist woman, jerked him out of the way. With all this justifica-
tion he opened his mouth and bawled.

"Oh, I'm really sorry!" the little woman apologized. What was
the matter with her, barging into people, endangering children?
She never acted that way!

"I'm so sorry," she said again. "Could I buy him an ice-cream
cone?"

"He's fulla ice cream, that's whatsa matter with him," the
mother replied. "Anyway, I got popcorn. Dannie, cut it out!"

The little woman started at the name, then covered the
movement with a gesture toward her hat. But the mother
hadn't noticed.

"We're gonna take the boat ride. I wanta see them educational
sights. I put in all year chasin' kids, now I'm gonna enjoy myself
if it kills me. Dannie!"

Yanking her screaming son after her, she charged off into
the crowd. Her bag of popcorn broke open, dropping a trail
of white kernels as if she were a fairy-tale character bound to
mark her way back.

The small woman stepped to the curb where she could stand
for a minute to catch her breath. She had felt so anonymous,
coming here on this secret little mission — so secret she hadn't
even made up her mind yet whether to see Diane this time —
and it had been shocking, in a way, to hear her own name
blurted out of the crowd. Not that the name had been addressed
to her. But now she had a sense of urgency she hadn't had
before. If someone were to come along who really knew her,
there would be at best a delay while she smiled and explained
how she had just happened to drop into town. And if the
person also knew Diane — one of the student nurses from St.
Matthew's, for instance — that would be even worse. How could
she say, don't mention this meeting to my niece because if my
suspicion is right then I wouldn't dare go near her. . . .

The suitcase skidded down rattling against the lamppost. Dannie opened the old black purse, took out a clean handkerchief and pushed up her hat. The hat left her forehead with a sticky little break. It would be pressing a red rim below her hairline. Carefully she wiped her brow. A few people were doing that, mostly men. They would think she was hot, if they thought at all. The cold clamminess of fear was as foreign here as the winter snows.

She put away the handkerchief. She was in front of the great building owned by the boat company, a cavernous affair architecturally somewhere between a mausoleum and a railroad station. If people were not hurrying in they were hurrying out. Between this edifice and the roller rink there was a gap of a quarter of a block where the sidewalk became a gallery topping the retaining wall. A crowd hung on the railing, looking down on another throng in the miniature park below. There would be an excursion boat loading at the dock for the moonlight trip up the river. With the departure of the boat most of the crowd would straggle away. Quickly, Dannie picked up the suitcase.

At the very corner of the boat company's building the long stairs began, plodding in low, wide steps down into the paper-strewn, smudgy park. Halfway down Dannie stopped. The statues were still there, close in by the wall, mummies of mud and shadow; but she couldn't take time to look at them now. Over on the riverbank, under the glare of the raw electric bulbs stringing together the docks and the ticket booth, there were clots of people. The big white excursion boat was in a frenzy of light and fluttering banners. The whole place was bright, almost fearfully so because the brilliance washing over all the faces touched her own.

Dannie leaned hard against the railing, her neck stretched tense as if every inch nearer might help, and her eyes cut into the crowd, slipping over the women, not even seeing the children, clinging for a second or two to every man. It was difficult to follow them, shifting as they did — almost like viewing the designs in a kaleidoscope and thinking surely you had seen that bit before. Down the ticket line face by face, across the scattered groups and the moving couples her gaze paced along, discarding everyone. She couldn't be quite positive about the people on the boat. With the distance, even though the deck was wide open to the sky, it was hard to tell exactly. But as the last few straggled past the ticket taker her confidence flared into open bloom. He was *not* here! She had been mistaken in believing she had seem him before. If she hadn't gone scuttling off like a scared rabbit, she would have sorted away those imagined similarities, *known* that this was the last place in the world he would ever be. And she would have saved herself three weeks of utter misery.

Almost weak with relief, Dannie turned slowly away from the bright lights. No reason now why she should not get a better look at the mud figures. They had intrigued her on that previous visit, but the first throbs of apprehension were driving through her then and she had thought of little else. Deliberately she crossed to the small, roped-off area and set down the suitcase. How nice that no one had destroyed the statues, for they were oddly beautiful even though they were only made of mud. Not perfect, any of them, but all so right, exactly what you might expect to find by a river. There was a drowned woman still clutching her baby, and a bearded riverman who had thrown himself down to sleep — you could actually see the difference between the sleeping and the dead — and a camp cook squatted beside his fire. A dog lay curled around her two small puppies. There had been more than the two in the beginning. That was why the mother was so protective toward these. The sculptor, whoever he was, possessed real talent to be able to express such delicate shadings through the ugly medium of mud. And he had revealed something of himself in his work. Tenderness, for instance, in the guarding pose of the dog's head, in the curve of the woman's arm about her child. But there was impatience, too. A face, nicely started, was caved in by a big footprint. Several mounds showed the first forming of hands or heads. Why had he not broken down these attempts and used them over instead of digging up new earth? The digging must be laborious. He had few tools, merely a spade, a bucket of water, several small instruments that looked like nut picks.

Dannie's little imaginings stumbled and fell apart. As one knows instinctively at times, she knew that someone was watching her. Nothing to be alarmed about, of course. She did have a few acquaintances in the Narrows. Casually she turned to the stairs, glancing over the crowd. Her glance did not go far. Like her thoughts a moment ago, it stumbled and stood still.

It was not he, she told herself numbly, it couldn't be. This was a stranger. The face was different. But not the eyes. Only one pair of eyes in the world could induce the beat of fear that leaped thumping against her ribs. They had not always looked at her that way. She had seen them laughing, impudent, pleading once in a while; but now they nailed her to the ground, cold and bleak, daring her to remember. I don't remember, she wanted to cry out, I don't know you, all I want is to get away and forget I ever saw you . . . let me go. . . .

She managed, somehow, to bend and pick up the suitcase. Yet how could she run? A woman chasing up the stairs, banging people with her suitcase, would stick out like a sore thumb in this leisurely crowd. Remember how conspicuous she had made herself up on Main Street! But she could leave, quietly, taking her time, and even if he should follow her — the thumping nearly overcame her — if he should follow her, what, after all, could he do? Nothing, if she remained with people. And she could sit on the green bench for the entire night if necessary.

With all the bravery she could muster, Dannie raised her head. And then she knew that fear was not only a lonely emptiness in the middle of the night. In that moment it became for her a cold gray thing against the heat and color of the carnival — a pair of eyes forbidding her to move or think or even breathe. And they blocked her only escape, the long stairs up to Main Street.

Down on the dock where the big white *Triton* was taking on her eight o'clock load of passengers a girl leaned back against the railing, one red sandal hooked into the bars behind her, her dark eyes eagerly upon the crowd. She never grew tired of watching people. In one way, vacationers were like the patients in the hospital, a tribe in themselves, cut off from the groove in which they spent their daily lives, and it was interesting to try to discern the marks of the groove. She was always doing that at St. Matt's, picking out the lawyers and shoe clerks and teachers, and then during the chitchat of nursing care she could find out if she was right. There was no way of finding out, here. Not that it mattered. She could always move on to a new face. That woman, for instance.

The woman had come into view at the top of the long stairs, a tiny person, not very well dressed, eye-catching because she carried a suitcase which in spite of its small size appeared to be quite a burden for her. Why hadn't she checked it at her hotel? the girl wondered idly. It would just be in her way on the boat ride. But perhaps she was not planning on taking the excursion for she came slowly, finally stopping to study the crowd. Even at that distance something about her was familiar. The girl unhooked her sandal from the rail and spoke to the blue-uniformed young man who was taking tickets at the gangplank.

"I'm going over there a minute, Ted."

"We're ready to pull out. Don't go far, Liz."

"I'll be right back."

The little woman had come on down the stairs to stand looking at the mud figures, so intent that she was entirely unaware of being an object of interest herself. Lizette approached the bed of drooping cannas. From here she could see the woman's face plainly. Somewhere they had met, herself and this little stranger, possibly at the hospital. Her cotton dress fitted her badly, and all you could say about her hat was that she had done the best she could with it. Her stockings were cheap but gartered up nice and tight so they only wrinkled slightly around the ankles. There was no permanent in her limp, soft hair, and she was alarmingly pale.

But she was beautiful. The goodness in her face shone forth like another light, surrounding her with the spiritual cleanness of a saint. There was fragility about her, too, a delicateness that called out for protection in this every-man-for-himself sort of world. You wanted to take her hand and pat her on the shoulder and assure her that things were going to be all right, if they weren't already. And things were not all right. The woman was worried, and worry had taken away her appetite, and lack of food had made her pale. Tiny lines of distress showed around her eyes and her lips had a tired sag. Lizette's mother feelings boiled up. Ted was always laughing at her for feeding stray cats and giving dimes to bums. But this woman was worthy of at least a kind word. Something about the mud figures, that would be a good opener, and then haven't-we-met-before. Somewhere, Lizette knew, she had seen that high-crowned hat with the three pink roses. There couldn't be another like it.

Lizette had stepped forward and was about to speak when a sudden, startling change came over the small stranger. She had been standing with the quietness of keen attention as she studied the statues; but now, as if she had received a physical blow, she stiffened. Her face became a death mask. For half of a frozen minute she did not move. Then, seemingly impelled by some force she could not resist, she turned toward the long stairs and again stood still.

In bewildered wonder Lizette scanned the crowd for some person or thing to account for this amazing change. But so far as she could see there was nothing fearful anywhere. Several people appeared to be watching the little woman, a natural consequence in view of her behavior; but none with lethal interest. Over on the stairs, a step or so up, was a garish figure in black Turkish trousers, white satin shirt, and orange turban — the mind reader who held forth in the purple tent up by the roller rink. Jinny was always going to him. A ludicrous creature, really. A little nearer, a paunchy tourist had planted himself, hat on the back of his head and jaw swinging around a half-eaten cigar. Very much diverted by the woman, Lizette thought fleetingly, but certainly not contemplating bodily harm. The neatness of his short beard was a contradiction to his general air of carelessness. The sculptor of the mud figures had appeared also, probably from a lair under the steps for he looked as if he had been heavily asleep a minute ago. He was a handsome animal of a man, tall and broadly built, his black shirt open far down over a powerful chest, graying hair tumbled back from a broad forehead, his whole bearing that of a vagrant. Lazily his gaze slid from the woman and came to rest on Lizette. In haste she looked away. Don't have anything to do with the carnival drifters, Ted was always telling her, keep clear of them. There was amusement in his smile, even derision, but nothing sinister. The only real animosity came from a frowsy, redheaded woman who glowered frankly and blocked the path to the stairs with the wide, solid stance of a man; but since she was glowering at everyone it was hard to tell how much of her

ill will was directed at the little stranger. Which of these people, Lizette mused, which is the alarming one? Or was it someone she hadn't noticed. . . ?

Down at the dock the *Triton* gave a warning toot. If Lizette
were to help the woman at all, it would have to be immediately.
She stepped forward and laid her hand on the shoulder of the
cotton dress.

"I'm sure we've met somewhere," she said. "At St. Matt's?
I'm a student nurse."

The woman spun to face her. For a fraction of a second
Lizette was certain she saw recognition in the really beautiful
blue eyes. But a hand went to the trembling mouth, cutting
off a very audible gasp; and then with the suitcase batting her
knees at every step, the little woman darted around the glowering redhead and rushed up the stairs.

Lizette could only stare after her in complete astonishment.
Surely she herself was not a frightening sight, yet the woman
was scrambling up the stairs as if her life depended on it. Side-
stepping away from the mind reader, she stumbled on to the
top and disappeared in the crowd.

"Friend of yours?"

Lizette jumped. The artist had come closer and was regarding
her with a very charming and very personal smile, most apprecia-
tive of her young slenderness and her summer tan and her dark
hair blowing in the wind. She could feel the catalogue being
made. Raising her chin high, she looked him up and down.

"I don't believe it's any concern of yours," she said. He
cocked his head as if he might be a little hard of hearing; but
she wouldn't repeat her statement, and then turning she walked
slowly past the canna bed.

The *Triton's* whistle jerked an insistent summons, but Lizette
would not hurry. That mud-pie character was not going to think

she was running away from him. She arrived on the dock just
as Ted began to lift the gangplank.

"Holy smoke, Liz, will you straggle aboard!" he urged. "You
know how Jerry is! What kept you?"

"I'm sorry, Ted, honestly I am," she said. Jerry, the *Triton's*
pilot, was old and a stickler for promptness because he wanted
to get home to bed. The guides were not supposed to take their
girl friends free on the boat rides, but all of them did it. Jerry
only put up with her presence, Lizette knew, because she never
bothered him. "I won't be late again," she promised.

"Maybe there won't be any again. He's mad."

Meekly, Lizette slipped past to stand beside the rail. Ted
slammed the gangplank into place and shouted to the pilot, and
the boat eased away from the landing. She fully expected Ted
to stride off forward, then, and take his place on the high stool
where he perched for his discourse to the passengers. Instead
he stopped beside her, looking straight ahead, his profile solidly
masterful as Caesar on a Roman coin.

"What did he say to you?"

"Who?"

"Don't hedge. That whole carnival outfit is a bunch of tramps!
Why did you go over there, anyway?"

"The woman. I thought I knew her."

"Was he asking you for a date?"

"Ted, really! You haven't any right to . . ."

"Haven't I? Whose frat pin are you wearing?"

Lizette slipped her hand under his elbow. There was no
response.

"Jinny thinks he's wonderful," she said, putting a smile into
her voice.

"Tell Jinny to keep away from him! He's no good!"

"All right, Jasper."

"What woman?"

"Just someone I noticed in the crowd."

"Why bother about her?"

"Because she interested me! Don't you ever wonder about people?"

"Sure. When I'm helping lay 'em out at Waddy's. You ought to see 'em sometime."

Lizette jerked her hand away.

"We gotta guide this trip or ain't we?" Jerry's voice came over the mike.

"Be seein' you," Ted muttered, and dived off into the twilight under the awning.

It wasn't what he had said about Waddy's, Lizette pondered furiously, it was the implication. He had become very insistent lately that she go with him to the mortuary. At a nice, quiet time, he said, when there was no one around. He hadn't exactly fancied his job as night man at first, either, he always explained; but it was good experience for a future doctor, and it fitted nicely into the night hours after he had finished on the boat. And a nurse who was expecting to be a doctor's wife would have to get over her aversion to seeing the dead because dying, he always ended up, was as natural as being born. A trip to Waddy's would be the first step in the getting-over process.

"Well, I'm not going," Lizette said aloud, and folded her arms firmly on the rail. "Ever," she added.

Wearing his fraternity pin didn't mean she had to knuckle under to Ted. She was going to keep the pin. And she wasn't going to Waddy's. And she was going to talk to whoever she pleased down on the water front, man or woman.

The lights of the town seemed to be receding while the boat stood still. Back there, somewhere, probably up on Main Street, the woman would be plodding along with her lonely little fears.

Surely, Lizette worried, there was something she could have done to help. Maybe tomorrow . . .

"Good evening, ladies and gentlemen," Ted began through the mike. "You are about to see the Narrows by moonlight, an unforgettable sight. We are now entering the Jaws of the Narrows. . . ."

The jaws of rock, standing out against the moonlight, looked savage. How long had they guarded the river? Against their age the span of a human life was a mere second — but still important to eternity. Tomorrow, Lizette promised herself, she would haunt the water front until she found the little woman again and she would make her understand her desire to help. And she wouldn't tease Ted any more. He was too wonderful a guy. But she wasn't going to Waddy's.

Dropping her cheek on her folded arms, she watched the path of moonlight spinning out behind the boat on the water. Life, she felt, was a very nice proposition.

Chapter Two

REACHING the top of the stairs, Dannie struck off blindly into the crowd. It didn't matter where she went. There was an awful giddiness swirling up somewhere out of the middle of her into her head so she felt as if she were staggering heavily yet floating at the same time. Something tapped at her brain like fate knocking at the door — but that would be the three pink roses bouncing on the hat. She must sew them down tighter. Diane would have a needle . . .

She stopped dead still. She could not go to Diane. She could not go because the worst had happened. She had met him. Face to face. And she had known him. And he had known her.

And then she had been confronted by the girl. That incident was a tag end, really, when you considered the terrible significance of the first. Yet you never knew into what importance a small beginning might grow. Lizette hadn't remembered her, quite, but she would. And what would be more natural than to ask Diane, at breakfast perhaps, if she had had a nice visit with Aunt Dannie. And Diane would be puzzled and hurt, and Lizette would recall how Aunt Dannie had been scared to death and gone scuttling away into the night, and there would be questions — why had her aunt been so frightened, why hadn't she come to Diane, where was she now . . . ?

"Oh, dear!" Dannie whispered. Her hand went up to the hat and the old black purse whacked to the pavement. Retrieving it, she was bumped by a man who said, "Excuse me" and three teen-agers who did not. She couldn't stand here in the street. Gripping the suitcase, she hastened up the long hill.

Movement was good for it gave her the illusion that she was doing something. But she couldn't rush hither and yon all night. Her heart was pounding, her breath short, and worst of all she was leaving the crowd behind. She stopped, gazing up the hill. A block or so ahead, above the softly rounded trees, sharp old-fashioned turrets stuck up against the sky. They were familiar turrets, in a way. She passed that place on the bus every time she came to town . . . Henry Waddy's mortuary . . . Henry! Why hadn't she thought of him before? Henry was used to counseling people in trouble, he would be calm and fatherly. Whether he would realize the significance of her discovery, that was something else. She would deal with Henry's possible doubt when the time came.

Nearly running, Dannie started ahead. Her arm was sore from lugging the suitcase. If only she could check it somewhere! She paused, glancing back down the hill. She had just passed a laundromat. They would have shelf room, they were used to bundles. Edging to the door, she looked inside. A man sat on a high stool with a newspaper spread out on the counter before him. On benches at the back of the long narrow room a dozen or so women flipped through magazines while their laundry did itself in the white machines ranged around the walls.

Dannie opened the door. The man laid down the paper. He had very clean hands.

"Hi," he said. "You come at the right time. I got a couple machines empty."

"Oh, I don't want to wash anything!" She hoisted the suitcase to the counter and tapped its shabby paper side. "Could I leave this with you? For an hour or so?"

The man rubbed the back of his neck. He was almost bald but on top of his head was a tiny patch of hair which he had parted in the middle. It gave him a dapper air.

"Well, I guess I can oblige. If you're comin' right back, that is. We don't make a practice of checkin' parcels."

"Oh, I am! And I'll pay you for your trouble, of course."

"No trouble. But I close at eleven."

The clock on the wall showed only a little after nine.

"I'll be here long before eleven," Dannie promised.

He pushed forward a tag and a pencil. "Name, please, lady."

"I'll be here," she repeated, nodding brightly, and hurried out into the street.

She was a little surprised at herself. There was no reason why she should not have given her name. Perhaps caution was being born of fear. She even peered back over her shoulder as she started up the hill under the dark maples. Henry's place, luckily, was only a few minutes away.

Dannie always knew that Henry Waddy had done well for himself. Except for the sign, *Funeral Home,* his establishment might easily be mistaken for another of the old but comfortably spacious residences of the neighborhood. Venetian blinds slit the view of lighted rooms within. There were geraniums in the window boxes with vinca vines trailing their green and white leaves. Hydrangea and bridal wreath and honeysuckle bulked against the white walls. A green rubber runner led from the street up to Henry's door where a rubber mat said *Welcome.*

Standing on the mat, Dannie pressed the doorbell. Soft chimes sounded inside. Perhaps Henry himself would open the door. He might not know her just on the instant. But it would take him no time at all to remember.

The door opened. Dannie's flicker of expectation died; for it was not Henry who stood on the threshold. This man was younger, tall and thin and stoop-shouldered. Never had she seen so bald a head. Down around his collar where it did nothing for his appearance he had a fringe of hair, but over the skull there was none. The light above him skated across a dome as shiny as the doorknob. He inclined his head and the light slid back.

"Good evening, Madam."

"Good evening. Is — I'd like to see Mr. Waddy, please."

"Mr. Waddy is not in. Perhaps I could help you?"

Dannie's heart sank.

"I make arrangements in Mr. Waddy's absence," the man added. "Of course, later you may talk with him. He always sees personally to all of our services."

"Oh, I — I'm not a customer!" Dannie said quickly. "No, Mr. Waddy is a friend — a friend of the family. I'm sure he'd see me!"

"Indeed, yes." His manner became slightly less formal. "I didn't quite understand. But Mr. Waddy really is not in. He left only a few minutes ago on a call. He doesn't go out any more, as a rule, but these people asked specially for him, and in such a case he never refuses. Mr. Waddy is very considerate toward the bereaved."

"I'd expect so," Dannie said. Henry would be like that, considerate toward everyone. Toward her, too. "Could I come in and wait? I wouldn't care how long!"

The man had nice eyes and they lingered on her in sympathy. "I'm sorry, madam, but I'm afraid it wouldn't do a bit of good. The place is far out, an hour each way — they can't drive fast, you know. It will be close to midnight when they get back and I'm sure Mr. Waddy won't return here. He'll have the driver drop him off at home. By that time Ted — our night man — will be here to help with the unloading."

"I see."

Dannie turned back down to the green matting. She had never felt more desolate in all her life. Behind her there was the soft twang of a spring as if the man had opened the screen door wider, and his voice was quick with concern.

"Couldn't you stop by in the morning? Mr. Waddy is always here around nine."

Morning was a night away, and fear nipped at her heels like a hound out of the dark. She murmured yes, she'd stop by in the morning, but the man must not have heard.

"Mr. Waddy will be asking who called, Madam. What name shall I say?"

Dannie increased her pace, pretending not to hear his question. She reached the end of the green rubber and turned once again toward the distant bright lights of Main Street.

She walked very fast, going downhill. There was one other possible source of help: Vince. He would *have* to come to her rescue. Not that she doubted his willingness. Quite the contrary. The difficult part would be to keep him from flying into instant action, calling the police, chasing down to the water front, embroiling everyone in wild confusion. Well, what if she couldn't restrain him? What difference would it make? At least the awful weight would be off her shoulders.

The jukeboxes were still making a gay affair of the evening when Dannie came again into the midway but she scarcely heard them. Just beyond the laundromat she crossed through the traffic, hurried on until she came to the bank corner, paused briefly, then sped off into the dark. If she remembered the location of Vince's house correctly, she wouldn't have far to go. Half a block later she saw that she had not forgotten, except that she was on the opposite side of the avenue. There could be no mistaking the place, bare of trees on a tree-lined street, a tall unlovely hulk making no pretense of being a home. Vince Barron never had cared about comfort. You'd never guess, looking at the house, that he had made a million in the lumber business. He must still have his offices crammed on to the lower floor, for the windows were dark. Upstairs, where he had always lived, one broad uncurtained window was lighted.

Eagerly Dannie came out to the curb, ready to cross. But then she stopped. A man had appeared in the window, a tall rangy man with a handful of papers which he began to flip one by one onto some surface below the sill. Twice as she watched he made quick dips out of sight, most likely to snatch at a paper that had gone sailing. Impatient, stormy Vince. Was he the one to trust with a secret which required calm deliberation?

"I don't know!" she whispered. "I don't know!"

But of course she did know, and the knowledge kept her from crossing the avenue and climbing those dark steps. She couldn't send Vince rushing around with a hotheaded charge of murder, not unless she was very sure. And was she that sure?

Slowly Dannie turned once again toward Main Street. She was so tired now that she could scracely drag one foot after the other. Better go to the hotel. But she had so little money. And if she were to remain in town — rather, since she *must* remain in town long enough to clear up this matter, then she dared not be extravagant. There was the practical certainty, too, that Lizette would mention something to Diane about having seen her aunt, and the only way to keep Diane from feeling hurt would be to go out to the hospital. It would conserve the small funds in the old black purse. And when you came right down to it, where was the danger — yet? She hadn't given herself away — at least, she hadn't spoken to him. He knew her, but how could he be sure that she knew him? And why exactly should he fear her? When she hadn't gone to the police twenty years ago, why should she go now?

A bus came just as she reached the bank corner and she sprinted to catch it. It had carried her on to the river bridge before she remembered the suitcase. She jumped up and staggered to the front of the bus. "I — I forgot something. How soon would I get a bus going back?" she asked the driver.

"That'll be me, lady." He looked at his watch. "Ten twenty-six now. It'd be about eleven. I go clear to the Heights before I turn around. Want me to stop?"

Dannie peered out into the black night. The laundromat would close at eleven. And besides, she shouldn't walk in on Diane any later than this.

"How's about it, lady?"

"No, I'll go on to St. Matthew's Hospital. Thank you."

Tomorrow morning, on her way to Henry's, she would stop and pick up the suitcase.

The corner where the bus stopped was well lighted. The hospital, too, was checked with lighted windows and there was a mellow flood around the entrance. But between, for half a block, lay nothing but darkness. Dannie would have to walk through it. Or run. For a panicky moment after she alighted she thought of shouting after the bus, making that friendly young man take her with him to the end of the line and back. But what good would that do? The hour would be later on the return. Go ahead, *now!* And walk, don't run. There was nothing to be afraid of. After all, the only difference between night and day was that you could see things in the daytime. At night you couldn't see . . .

But you could hear.

There were steps behind her. Long steps. Keeping the rhythm of her own. But catching up to her because of that long stride. Only a man would pace along like that.

Only a man. And the sheltering trees made a black tunnel ending a lifetime away at the hospital entrance.

Chapter Three

LIZETTE, rocking the baby, hummed softly to him. In the shadowy room seven other babies slept in their cribs. This was her favorite time in the routine of pediatrics. The uproar caused by the departure of parents was long past and all but the most restless children were settled for the night. Life in general was a very satisfactory proposition. Ted had been nice to her on the boat ride after he had worked off his ire over the sculptor, and they had made a date to go up the river to their favorite picnic spot and cook breakfast. Morning dates were different. And practical. Ted was always being practical. That was why he couldn't understand her phobia about going to Waddy's.

The baby grunted, pushing the bottle away.

"Full up, Butch?" Lizette whispered. "O.K., we'll cuddle. But don't breathe a word of it to Sister Simon."

She laid the baby against her shoulder and patted him softly. A student nurse appeared in the doorway.

"Liz?"

"All right, Jinny, tell Simon I'll be there."

"She didn't send me. I had to tell you, I got my time off!"

"For the whole Festival?"

"Ya, the whole three days! Sister Pete didn't say a thing.

I've got to make up the time, of course. That's what I'm doing now, I should of been off at eleven. But I don't care! I don't care about nothin' as long as I can be queen!"

"Hey, don't wake up the kids," Lizette cautioned, but she did it gently. In Jinny's drab life there had been one beautiful, cherished honor. Up in the woods last summer in her home town of Marshlands, population six hundred twenty-nine, she had been elected Blueberry Queen. Next week, courtesy of Sister Peter, she would return to Marshlands for a brief reign before passing her crown on to the new queen.

Jinny doubled down on a chair and hooked her elbow awkwardly over the back. It was easy to imagine Jinny at the age of eighty with the same tired droop and the same bowed shoulders, for the hard work she had been obliged to do throughout her childhood had made an old woman of her. And she was never really neat. Even in the immaculate pink uniform and white apron, with her long blond hair netted, she managed to have a tousled air. That she remained in nursing school at all was a tribute to the ability of her classmates to cover up her mistakes. Other classes knitted for the lepers or adopted babies in the Far East as their projects. This one looked out for Jinny.

"Liz, you don't think it's funny, do you?"

"What's funny?" Lizette asked, absently because she was running over the possible blunders Jinny might have made since coming on duty at seven. Probably none. Anybody could tuck the kids in for the night. "What do I think is funny, Jin?"

"Me being queen."

"Of course not!"

"The others do. They think I'm too dumb to catch on, and mostly I am, so how can I help being calm as a cucumber? But I dunno. . . ." Jinny twisted around into another awkward attitude and a forlorn note crept into her voice. "It makes me feel like the fun I had being queen, it wasn't really fun at all and maybe people were laughing at me. But you never laugh, Liz. You're just wonderful to me."

"I'm always wonderful to my roommates," Lizette said. Jinny's outbursts of devotion were sometimes burdensome. "Listen, go rinse this bottle if you want something to do."

"Is that Randy?"

"Mm-hm."

"I don't see why you fed him when I just got through."

"You just — oh, Jin, you didn't!"

"Isn't he a ten o'clock feeder?"

Count ten, Lizette told herself, take it easy. Evidently Jinny had not looked at the feeding board; and having fed the baby, she hadn't charted it. Two large blunders right there.

"Liz, if Simon finds out she'll have me campused! I won't get to the Blueberry Festival! I'll even get kicked clear out of school!"

"If you're kicked out you'll have plenty of time to be queen!" Lizette snapped. "And you might give a thought to Randy. After all, he's in here for regulation of his formula!"

Jinny by now was crying into her apron, muttering her contrition. The baby seemed happy. Could it be possible Jinny's mistake had uncovered the answer to his finicky appetite, feed him in two courses instead of one?

"Are you going to tell Sister Simon?"

"Why shouldn't I?" Lizette retorted, but at Jinny's wail she added quickly, "All right, I won't. I'll chart it all as one feeding. But for Pete's sake pay attention to what you're doing! And stop bawling! If Simon sees you like that she'll want answers you'll never think up!"

"Do the charting quick, Liz!"

"Well — I'll see."

Lizette, hurrying down the hall to the nurses' station, reflected that someone, sometime, should permit retribution to catch up

with Jinny. Why not now? Of late she had been more careless
than ever. It might do her good to be given a thorough scare
on the eve of her great day, since no amount of lecturing seemed
to impress her. And the baby, too, might benefit if it were known
how he had enjoyed his supper.

But when Lizette saw Sister Simon bent wearily over the
desk, her pretty, young face drawn with fatigue, the determina-
tion left her. The Sister was peckishly strict, often a peevish
disciplinarian because she was very little older than the students
herself. Yet she would give in to the parents when she should
have been firm. Overworked, of course, but that seemed to be
the normal state for the nuns in the hospital. She shouldn't
even be here, close to midnight. The end of a sixteen-hour day,
Lizette decided, was no time to present anyone with an incident
which called for extreme forbearance. She reached for Randy's
chart. Just this once — but never any more — she would cover
up for Jinny.

The telephone rang. Still writing, the nun lifted the receiver,
said "No!" with severity, and hung up. Lizette turned the pages
of the chart slowly. Why should she think the call had been
for her? Ted would know better than to ring the floor. And
her family was three hundred miles away. In case of emergency
Sister Simon would let her take a call. It couldn't have been
anything of importance, most likely not even for her. Yet the
stiffness of the nun's back gave her the uneasy impression of
resistance. The little office was so quiet that the electric clock,
shifting its minute hand, made quite a small disturbance.

Sister Simon frowned hard at the work schedule before her.
She was not going to pass the message on to Lizette. She was
too busy. People should not call at this hour. She moved her
head from side to side, trying to relax. Since she had become

a supervisor she was always tired. If only she could have a short vacation! But in the convent there were few vacations. If you had your shoes on you carried your full load.

And the load, today, had been heavy. Johnny Phelps's mother, for one thing, demanding a certain crib for her son. And getting it. Sister Paul would never have yielded. But Sister Paul was older, she knew how to handle people. Upsets were always happening on pedes. No use pretending she didn't feel the burden of her youth and inexperience; but it was Mother's wish that Sisters be supervisors wherever possible, and since there were not enough nuns ever to go around and Sister Simon had passed her registry with a nearly perfect mark and she loved children, it was inevitable that she be made supervisor of pediatrics.

The neat writing began to swim. She lifted her face to the open window. Lizette had finished her charting and gone. The warm summer night sent in its sounds — the disharmony of the midway across the river, faint and toylike; the whistles of the boats, an automobile humming by; and under it all the vast quiet that was the night itself. Life was like that, a medley of annoyances but with certainty underneath. Never in the least confused as to her religious vocation, she had allowed the human irritations of supervising to beat her down. To keep peace she had given in to Mrs. Phelps. When an aide had telephoned, late, that she would be absent from duty there was no reprimand although these absences always coincided with some escapade of her worthless husband. One thing after another kept cropping up to break down discipline. Like Evvie's call a few minutes ago. Evvie knew the rules perfectly well. They were posted right above the switchboard.

Thrusting her pen into the red ink, Sister Simon reached for a slip of paper and with a force that spread the pen point she printed in large letters, "ATTENTION." The telephone rang. She took it up, listened, and a flush of annoyance warmed her cheeks.

"Why do I have to tell you this again, Everine? Visiting hours are over at nine. And you know perfectly well that the students do not receive visitors on duty."

I shouldn't be explaining, Sister Simon thought. She cut into Evvie's apologetic pleading.

"Certainly you can tell the woman that! Why not?"

She dropped the receiver into place. Evvie would not have given Sister Paul any argument. With herself, from now on, it would be the same. A rule was a rule and every single one would be kept. She took up the pen again, carefully recrossing the t's. A dear little person, Evvie had said, and something about Diane being out on a date and so the woman was asking for Lizette.

"Ambulance just pulled in," Mrs. Popnesky announced, trudging into the chart room. "Wanta bet we get it?"

"I'd probably lose."

"That kind of a night, huh?"

Sister Simon nodded and crumpled up the paper, for she had absently drawn a villainous face in the letter O. The wad hadn't hit the wastebasket before the phone rang again. Poppy reached for it.

"We better turn down the bed in 32," she said before she answered. "I'm gonna win the bet."

Sister Simon felt herself smiling. Poppy had that effect on people. Her hair was usually stringing out and her cap had been seen to wear a dash of chocolate for a week, her slip hung down and her uniform hiked up in the back; but for dependability and cheer she had no equal.

"I toldya," she said. "Kid hit by a car. I better get movin'."

Sister Simon dropped the red pen. It would be a good deal

later that she would remember her irritation at Evvie's infringe-
ment of the rules — remember and wonder whether she herself
had actually measured out for someone the difference between
life and death.

Everine leaned out of her cubicle as far as the harness on
her head would permit. She dared not leave the switchboard
because the ambulance was screaming up the alley, but she did
look anxiously after the little woman. There was something
so very pathetic in the way she had asked so diffidently for
Diane, then for Lizette, accepting the discouragement as if she
really deserved nothing less.

"It's right there," Evvie urged. The woman glanced back. Her
cotton dress was crumpled, but the three roses stood up stoutly
against the crown of the hat. Evvie's finger poked the air.
"There! To your right. The light switch is right inside the
door."

"I'll find it. Thank you, dear."

She did go into the waiting room, but no light came on. The
room would not be completely dark, of course, for the archway
was wide open. Sit down and wait, Evvie had said, Lizette
will be down in a little while. A white lie, but what could
you do? What a time for Simon to stiffen her backbone! Which
was more important, anyway, the darn rules or this little scared
woman?

The switchboard buzzed and Evvie sat down to answer.
Emergency wanted things. It was several minutes before she
could peek around her corner again. Still there was no light in
the waiting room. Honestly! — the poor soul didn't have to sit
in the dark! Troubles looked bad enough with a lamp on. Evvie
lifted the headset carefully off the curls she had made blond
for the summer. She could scoot to the waiting room, turn
on a light, give the little woman a reassuring word which she

probably wouldn't believe, in view of everything, and be back inside a minute.

But with the headset in her hand, she paused. Up and over the archway which separated the hall from the lobby a Christmas ivy grew. Even in summer when the front door opened there was enough draft between the door and the freight elevator shaft to swing the delicate tendrils. They were swinging now. Evvie ran her hand around inside her belt to tuck in her blouse, lifted her bosom, and pulled in her stomach. She was "Information" at night and she had picked up some nice acquaintances here, particularly young men with mothers in the hospital.

A minute went by. No one appeared. Well, then the little woman must have gone out when the ivy swayed. There was another doorway, unseen from here, from the waiting room into the lobby. O.K., so she was gone. But the ivy began to swing again, gently. Now somebody would have to appear. Two people couldn't go out one after the other when there was only one to go in the first place.

Yet the hall remained empty. The switchboard buzzed. Mechanically Evvie capped the headset in place. Another buzzer joined the first.

"Oh, murder!" Evvie muttered, and flung herself into her chair. First chance she had, she was going to walk down the hall and look in the waiting room. If the woman was gone, fine, she'd forget about her.

But there was a flurry of calls and Evvie hadn't a minute to herself. When she heard footsteps beating hurriedly through the hall, she leaned out of her corner.

"Jinny? Hey, you're on pedes, aren't you?"

Jinny, almost by, kept stepping away backward.

"Yes. It's a little girl. I'm going to the blood bank."

"Listen, tell Liz to give me a ring right away, will you?"

"Maybe she won't even live."

"Jin, will you tell Liz? It's real important!"

"Tell her what?"

But already Jinny was running away.

Honestly! Evvie told herself bitterly, you'd think the fates were dead against the little woman. It would never do to ring pedes again and ask for Liz. She would have to count on way-laying Jinny on her return.

Jinny, however, must have taken the elevator over by emergency because the only human being to appear within the next ten minutes was a timid man who asked if it wasn't much too late for him to go up to see his wife.

Lizette glanced at her watch as she ran down the stairs. Nearly half past twelve. Call Evvie about something, Jinny had said, it's real important. Sister Simon was still on the floor so she didn't want to use the station telephone. The simplest thing was to run down to the switchboard.

"What does he want in the dead of night?" Lizette demanded almost before she was around the corner.

Evvie looked up from the confession magazine rolled open on her lap. "What he?"

"Ted. Didn't you tell Jinny . . ."

"Oh, not him. This woman. But she's gone now. I guess she didn't think it was any use her waiting."

"What woman, Evvie?"

"I dunno. She didn't seem to know you very well, just your first name."

"But if she asked for me . . . " Not the little woman from the park! With an odd sensation that reminded her of dread, Lizette pictured the small figure hurrying up the stairs to Main Street. "Didn't she tell you what she wanted, Ev?"

"No. She was scared about something, though. I sure wish

Diane had hit on some other night to take a one o'clock pass."

"Diane? Was it her aunt?"

"I guess so. Know her?"

"So that's who she was!"

"Come again?"

"Remember that tea the student nurses gave for their parents about three weeks ago? Diane brought her Aunt Dannie. She was better dressed that time, but she had the same hat. I knew I'd seen it before! Why didn't I think of it!"

"Did she go upstairs, after I went and told her. . . ."

"No, no, I saw her this afternoon. Tell me what she said to you, Ev."

"Not much. When I said Diane was out on a date, she asked for you. She sure needed somebody, I could see that. So how could I say Simon wouldn't co-operate, for gosh sake! Honest, that nun thinks being a supervisor is saying no all the time."

"What did she do then?"

"Slammed up the receiver."

"No — the woman!"

"Oh. Well, I said sit in the waiting room a while and Liz will be down. I was going to get you, too, if it was the last thing I ever did under this holy roof. And I bet it woulda been. I guess maybe she went in there for a minute, but then she left."

"Did you go look?"

"I didn't hafta. The ivy started swinging, you know how it does when the door opens."

Lizette started down the hall toward the waiting room.

"She's gone, Liz," Evvie said.

But the girl hurried on. The waiting room was empty. She turned into the lobby which was illuminated only by the patch of light striking in from the hall. The outer door was closed.

Opening it wide she stepped on the doorstop, pushed open the screen, and was outside.

The old lamp above the door was bleary, its globe dark with the moths that had fluttered themselves to death inside. The moonlight was almost brighter than the lamp. Leaning on the balustrade, Lizette looked down past the stone steps to the street. The little woman would have had to plunge into the darkness under the oaks, fly along with their leafy prattle surrounding her like enemy whispers. Evvie should have told her about the short cut through the basement, for the nurses' home was almost certain to be her destination.

Lizette ran down the stairs to the pavement to look in either direction. Silly, of course. Aunt Dannie would never dally here. By now she would be safe in Diane's room, probably sound asleep.

Lizette took a long breath of the sweet air. The nicotiana Sister Joe had planted in close to the building was perfuming the whole night. Against the dark wall the pale flowers were plainly visible. A few sprigs in a glass of water would do a lot for the nurses' station. The girl started up the rather steep terrace. And stopped.

Something had been tossed into the shadow of the wall. Something black. She had stopped because the thing was against her foot. She pushed it with her toe. It was light, moving easily. Slowly she bent to touch it — a black straw hat.

After a moment she straightened with the hat in her hand. It was an old-fashioned hat, high in the crown. Across the front were three roses. In the moonlight the roses were gray.

Chapter Four

LIGHTLY, Lizette touched the roses. The little woman must have lost her hat when she ran down the stairs. That was the logical explanation. But suddenly the girl wanted no more of the darkness. Clutching the hat she whirled, even took a long stride back down the terrace.

And that was when her gaze fell full upon the plum tree.

It was a peculiar tree, less than waist high even in maturity, the branches spread like an umbrella and bowed to the ground with green fruit. Small boys of the neighborhood, playing cowboy and Indian, often used it as a wigwam. Its shelter now was no part of a game. From under the wide fan of a limb a small foot protruded, a foot that she could see even in the poor light had on a worn black shoe. The stocking above the shoe would be wrinkled around the ankle.

Lizette stared at the foot. It was almost as if she expected to see it there and so she had no reaction at all. After a minute she moved slowly across the grass, bent, and touched the ankle. There was a spot right in front of the bone where you could feel for a pulse. If there was one. Her fingers explored. Then, still with that sensation of numbness she rose, walked to the steps and up, through the door, and into the lobby.

She knew exactly what to do in caring for the dead. Call
the intern, get the clothing list, put the belongings together
with the body on the stretcher, and cover it with a sheet —
only you did all that when the body lay decently in bed, not
sprawled with a twisted foot under a plum tree. . . .

Someone was holding her by the shoulders, pressing her so
hard against the archway that the ivy cracked behind her
spine.

"Liz, what in the dickens hit you?"

Her vision cleared. It was Merle, the curly-headed night
orderly, who was doing his best to ruin the ivy.

"You look like you've seen a ghost, kid. What's up?"

"The numbness broke and she sagged weakly down on the
edge of the jardiniere. Merle looked from her to the hat, then
caught it up on one finger and twirled it.

"Hey, quite a chapeau."

"Stop that!" Lizette clapped her hand over her mouth to
keep back the scream. Merle, with the hat at a tipsy angle,
stretched his neck in surprise. He looked very funny, like a
cartoon she had seen of a rooster swallowing a string.

"Listen, Merle," she said quietly, "there's a woman out on
the lawn. Dead. You'd better go quick before — before somebody . . . "

Before somebody what? Nothing could hurt the little woman
any more.

Evvie was there by now, backed against the wall, trembling,
her eyes wide as if the stiff lashes propped them open.

"Liz, our little lady? She isn't really — *dead?*"

"Yes." Lizette stood up, not even swaying. "Death is a natural
thing, perfectly natural. Go on, Evvie, call the intern. And
Father Paul."

The words didn't come out very well. But Merle went. Evvie,
too, for in a moment the speaker high on the wall gave the

small scratch of the switch being turned on and Evvie's voice came softly but urgently, "Dr. Barney. Father Paul." Now all would be done that could be done for the little woman.

Carefully Lizette walked to the freight elevator, opened the grating, pushed it shut behind her, and pressed her thumb on the third-floor button. She felt competent, no faintness, no confusion. The second floor slid down from above and slipped away below. She stopped at exactly the right instant and pulled open the grating.

And then, unaccountably, panic seized her. There was no reason for it by that time. The floor kitchen was black dark but quite familiar, the wide door to pediatrics a dimly lighted oblong. Lizette ran toward it, heard the buzzer in the elevator snappishly remind her that she had not closed the door, and stumbled as she turned back. The slam she gave the door was enough to shake the whole shaft. She didn't care. She couldn't hold back the storm inside her any longer.

By the time she reached the station she was crying in long sobs that sickened her and made a great deal of noise. Poppy, sitting pigeon-toed on a high stool, nearly fell headlong getting off. Sister Simon, at the desk, looked up. The pen fell from her grasp and made a big red blot on the white paper.

"It's your fault, Sister! All your fault!" Lizette sobbed, and she would have gone on except that her face was being pressed against Poppy's shoulder and Poppy's arms were very tight around her.

"Let's not wake every kid in the county," Poppy soothed, but there was alarm in her voice. "What you been up to, anyhow?"

"Ask Sister! She knows!"

Lizette heard the scrape of the Sister's chair being pushed back, then the rush of water at the sink. Shoving Poppy away, she confronted the nun.

"You couldn't let me go, could you, Sister, not even speak

to her on the phone, and I was sitting there, *right there,* when Evvie called! You wouldn't even tell me she was here!"

The water overflowed the glass, running down into the Sister's sleeve. She shut off the faucet and held out the glass to Lizette. The girl dumped it and slammed it upside down on the drainboard.

"Your rules are so important, aren't they? No visitors during duty, no leaving the floor except on necessary errands! Oh, we have the most law-abiding floor in the whole. . . . "

"Lizette!"

Lizette whirled to Poppy. "Since when is a rule more important than a woman's life?"

"What woman?"

"Aunt Dannie." She turned to the nun. "How are you going to tell Diane?"

"Tell her — what?" That was the first thing the Sister had said.

"That Aunt Dannie is dead. Somebody killed her."

"Somebody killed her? How?" Poppy gasped.

Lizette's tumbling thoughts stopped short. Why had she said Aunt Dannie was killed?

"I don't know. But you don't toss away your hat — your hat that you've fixed all up the best you can — and then crawl off under the plum tree and die! Not if you're scared to death of the dark in the first place!"

"Is that what . . . what she . . . "

"Yes, and if Sister had let me go, she might be alive right now!"

"All right, ducky," Poppy said in the tone she used for the children. "Let's not split our seams."

"You'd better get some seconal for her," Lizette heard the nun say, and her voice was strangled as if the coif had suddenly become too tight.

"Maybe she hasn't reported it, Sister. When you find a body you're supposed to . . . "

"I did, I told Evvie," Lizette managed to choke out, "but not Diane. She's out on a date!"

"Oh, lordy!" Poppy breathed. "Sister, we can't put this kid to sleep. The police will want to ask questions."

"They can question her tomorrow, nothing will be changed by morning."

You're so right, Lizette wanted to say, but what was the use? She had said a lot of things to the nun. Too many. But Sisters were human. If they made human mistakes, why shouldn't they bear the consequences?

Obediently the girl swallowed the capsule Poppy offered her. It was disgraceful, really, to go to pieces like this. How dependable would she be as a nurse if she became hysterical every time a patient died? But this was not just a patient, it was a poor creature she might have helped except for Sister Simon's stubborn regard for rules.

"Come on now, dearie," Poppy said. "Off to bed with you."

"You'll be alone on the floor, Poppy."

"In a manner of speaking, yes. But Jinny is here, remember."

Lizette knew Sister Simon watched them leave, and it seemed to her that she was still watching as they proceeded down in the elevator, through the basement, across the alley, and into the nurses' home. By that time the seconal was beginning to take effect. She was not going to dream of Sister Simon. Nor of Aunt Dannie, either. Dying was as natural as being born — Ted said so — only there was nothing natural about the foot sticking out from under the plum tree. . . .

The last thing she felt was her head falling against the pillow and someone lifting her feet up onto the bed.

Poppy remained with Lizette until she was certain the girl was asleep. The kid had had a terrific shock and somehow she had tied it all up with Sister Simon. A pretty unstable reaction, but then it wasn't every day you'd run into murder. . . .

"Murder?" Poppy quavered aloud.

Why had she put it that way when she'd have to scoot back across the dark alley alone! She peered out of the window. The moon had set. The hospital grounds were as black as the inside of Jonah's whale. She would run, fast, and nobody would have a chance to grab her. Lizette was breathing deeply, sound asleep. Go on now, before she lost her nerve.

Poppy slipped through the hall and in fear and trembling let herself out into the alley. She looked up and down. Once your eyes were used to the darkness it wasn't so bad. She could see the ladders stacked where the window washers had left them, the garbage cans over by the basement door. The whole bulk of the hospital stood between her and the front lawn. From the third-floor windows, of course, she could see perfectly well but it wouldn't be the intimate view she would have from the ground. Go around the building and there she'd be, screened by the lilacs, in a dandy position to see for herself what was going on around the plum tree.

It was even better than Poppy had expected. She could look out unseen right onto the terrace. There were men, half a dozen of them, and they were flashing lights all over. A photographer's bulb whitened the little tree for a split second, enough for Poppy to determine that no one now lay on the grass. They must have carried the woman into the hospital morgue. They kept their voices disgustingly low. All she could make out with any degree of certainty was that they were searching for a weapon and not finding one.

Quietly Poppy backed out of the lilacs and groped again toward the alley. If they were hunting a weapon then Liz was right, the woman had been killed. Murdered. And she was Diane's aunt. Poppy dredged up all the memories she had of the student nurses' relatives. They were sparse, mere greetings at Christmas parties. She should circulate more, then when something interesting like this came up she'd know. . . .

A loud, resounding clang echoed through the alley. Poppy shrank against the old bricks. She thought she screamed. In a single wild second she saw herself flat on the pavement in a pool of blood with a monster leering over her.

And then a cat yowled. The garbage cans, of course. She had surprised the scavenger at its nightly prowling. But she sprang for the door, yanked it open, and shot inside. That was the worst of murder, it wasn't inflicted upon the victim alone but upon every mortal and thing around it. Every small sound became the possible warning of danger. The cops hadn't found the weapon. Maybe the guy was stalking around in the dark, making ready to use it again. . . .

"Lordy, lordy, don't let him be in the elevator!" Poppy prayed frantically.

He was not. The grating stood open upon a lighted cage.

But next to the elevator was a small door, lower than most, with a pane of glass so thickly frosted that even when the room was lighted no one would see in. Behind the window was a glow of light. Only members of the staff were permitted in the morgue. But anyone else could go in if they felt like it, simply by opening the door.

Tiptoeing, Poppy approached the door. She touched the knob. In the same instant a man's shadow fell, black and giant, against the frosted glass. Poppy had not been awed by the morgue since her student days when she had stepped into the disinfected little place with such misgivings that she usually forgot to duck her head, and whacked it against the low lintel. The sight of the man's shadow hit her with the old impact of the lintel. She turned and ran.

Slamming the elevator door, Poppy flattened her thumb on

the button. Everywhere, in the dark rooms and corners and especially down below in the shaft where the dark mounted into a skyscraper as the elevator rose, there the murderer lingered. And every small creak of the cables was the same bugaboo that had cried with the cat.

"Lord, just let me make the third floor," Poppy prayed, "and I'll camp there the rest of my life!"

She put her hand to her tousled hair. Somewhere down in the dark she had lost her cap. The lilac branches had streaked the whole side of her uniform. She would indeed be a lovely sight for Sister Simon, the immaculate. But she had one point decidedly in her favor. She was alive.

Chapter Five

TED paused on the ramp that took the place of steps leading from the hall door down to the floor. He had been here several times but the room still intrigued him. Aside from the entrance and the extreme bareness, you wouldn't remark anything unusual about it. Knowing it was a morgue was what made the difference. A long table cluttered with beakers, not very clean, ended in a sink. In one corner of the room was a large partitioning which could have been a closet. Mr. Waddy, jogging down the ramp, nodded toward it.

"She'll be in the cooler, of course. Well. Close the door, Ted. Tightly."

The young man tried the already closed door. His shadow fell like a black giant on the frosted glass. Then, carefully, he let his stretcher roll before him down to the floor. Care was the watchword when the old gentleman was present. Mr. Waddy had just returned from a lengthy jaunt into the country when the call from the hospital came in. Ted had been surprised when Mr. Waddy, listening in at home, said he would accompany him. The mechanic who slept at the mortuary would have done as well. But the news of murder had apparently banished

any fatigue Mr. Waddy might have felt at the end of his eigh-
teen-hour day. Briskly he nodded to Ted and trotted over to
the bulletin board.

"Always take a look here first, son. Sometimes they post a
note for you. Although the body, of course, will be tagged."

"Yes, sir," said Ted. He knew these things. But it was Mr.
Waddy's way to educate a new man.

Amused, Ted watched the old gentleman push his good gray
hat to the rim of his gray curls, tip back his head, and bring
the bulletin board into range of his bifocals. Even in high
curiosity, he would never cut corners. He had found a note
and was perusing it thoroughly. A stranger guessing his business
would never have taken him for a funeral director. He was,
rather, a child's dream of a grandfather, lively of eye and limb,
short enough for his ear to be on easy level for whispered
secrets, plump enough to have a cuddly lap when he sat in a
rocking chair. His favorite Sunday pastime, so the boys said,
was to take his wife and the grandchildren on long walks to
gather wild flowers in the country. In his young days he had
preached in small country churches where they could not afford
a minister. A popular toastmaster for local banquets, he had
served also as chairman of the school board and had passed out
high school diplomas on every graduation night for twenty years.
It was all extremely good for business. People, bereaved, naturally thought of Mr. Waddy. And he was never a disap-
pointment.

Ted, lounging on the ramp, began to whistle absently. Mr.
Waddy turned in reproach.

"My boy, we are in the presence of the dead."

"Oh. Sorry."

"If I teach you nothing more, do remember in your future
practice of medicine that a dead body is not a thing, it is still
the God-made image of Himself and during its years of life

it housed a soul. Therefore it commands reverence. Right? Well."

Ted had been advised ahead of time about these little lectures and he had expected to find them very funny. They were not. He was even embarrassed enough to try to bring up some sort of apology. But the old gentleman would never permit any molehill of thoughtlessness to be made into a mountain. A correction, once over, was a closed incident.

He stepped across to the cooler.

"Allow me, sir."

Ted strode across the room, threw the heavy handle and swung back the door. The temperature, somewhere around forty degrees, felt like Antarctica after the heat. He took hold of the cart to shunt it out.

"Read the tag, son, read the tag," Mr. Waddy advised.

"O.K., sir. But there's only the one." Ted squinted briefly at the cramped writing. "Diana something. If you'll step back, sir, I'll get her out where there's more light."

It took him a minute to push out the cart and secure the door. When he turned Mr. Waddy, with the tag in his hand, had folded the sheet down as far as the little woman's shoulders and he was staring at her with a most amazed expression. The apples had faded entirely from his cheeks. The room was so quiet that a car, swooping through the alley with its horn blasting, sounded like a devil abroad from the underworld.

"Sir, do you — you don't know her?" Ted asked. "I mean, people that are murdered, you don't usually know them."

The white bosom of Mr. Waddy's shirt lifted and he laid a gentle hand on the sheet.

"Yes, I know — knew her. Dannie Grear."

For the first time Ted really looked at the woman. Where her dress showed above the sheet there was a drying dark red stain. Mr. Waddy examined it briefly.

"Stabbed. The hand that struck her down was a violent one. But she died without violence inside her. It's how I'd expect her to go."

He gave the arm another light pat, a gesture of comfort to himself, perhaps, since the little woman could not feel it. "But she shouldn't have had to go like this," he added. Then he laid the sheet back in place.

He was too old, Mr. Waddy often said, for the heavy lifting a mortician must do; yet now, although Ted was at his elbow, he wrapped the sheet tightly about the body and lifted it without aid to his own cart. Then he turned the cart so it would ascend headfirst. There was never any willy-nilly either-end-first with Mr. Waddy.

"We're ready, Ted. If you'll get the door . . . "

With one hand on the door, the other holding the head of the cart, the young man hesitated. "I'm sorry, sir. I mean, seeing her like this, if she was a friend, it's quite a blow."

Mr. Waddy nodded. "Quite a blow. Yes. Now let's be on our way, son."

They had good footing on the rubber matting which, Mr. Waddy said, had been his suggestion years ago, and the cart moved readily. Ted reached behind him to open the door. Swinging out, the door bumped someone who had been standing very close to it in the hall.

Sister Simon left the floor as soon as Poppy returned. Not that she felt like going to rest; but Poppy, with her usual tactlessness, would begin asking questions and the Sister had no answers. She stood a minute before she entered the freight elevator, hesitated again before she pushed the down button. She knew she was acting with unusual deliberation; but if she were to proceed with the haste that had become habit, then she might catch up with some of the things that were waiting for her to think about. Two floors slid up past the elevator. She hadn't intended, exactly, to go to the basement; yet, reaching it, she pushed back the grating and stepped out.

The place smelled of soap and food from laundry and kitchen, leftover workaday smells that made the total quiet more noticeable. Slowly the nun ascended the short stairs to the alley door and looked out. A few paces away across the pavement was the entrance to the nurses' home. Half a minute and she could be with Lizette. But what could she say? That nothing is more important than a rule?

"Her duty was on the floor, to me and to the patients!" the Sister whispered vehemently, and her fist struck the door. "I was doing my duty when I refused to let anything interfere! The woman had no business being where she was at such an hour with such a request. I couldn't foresee what would happen! I have to keep order."

Something moved out in the alley. A cat. She turned quickly away. Next to the elevator was the small door to the morgue. Light showed behind the frosted glass. They wouldn't be doing the autopsy on the woman yet, for the pathologist lived miles away. But someone was there. She could go in and look at the body herself. Then she might know whether a few seconds snatched in spite of a rule might have meant the difference between life and death. It would all depend on how the woman had died.

She laid her hand on the knob. From inside someone turned the knob and the door bumped her as it swung open. She was looking right into the face of a strange young man.

He was as startled as she. At the far end of the stretcher stood Mr. Waddy. In spite of her preoccupation the thought struck her forcibly that Mr. Waddy was getting on in years. Never had she seen him appear so tired. His face was almost as gray as the hat he held nipped against the stretcher.

He nodded politely. "Good evening, Sister Simon," he said, and gave her a kind little smile.

She forgot that the little smile was probably as professional a piece of garb as the striped trousers he wore at funerals. His kindness touched off a terrific urge to cry. Like the time she had cut her finger as a youngster and borne up bravely until her mother said, "Oh, you poor darling!" and the flood had come. To dam it back now, she said very stiffly,

"Good evening, Mr. Waddy."

He waited a moment, then said apologetically, "If we might proceed into the hall, Sister — the cart is a bit difficult to hold on the slant."

"Of course," the nun murmured and moved quickly out of the way. The young man was very competent. In a minute the cart was in the hall, the light off in the morgue and the door closed. Now they would be leaving, up the steep stone flight to the alley, and her only opportunity would be gone.

"Mr. Waddy?"

"A moment, Ted. Yes, Sister?"

"Mr. Waddy, was she — you don't know what happened to her, how she died?"

He shook his head gently. Then he took off his glasses and rubbed hard at the marks on his nose. Putting the glasses on again, he inspected the front of the Sister's apron.

"That is for the coroner to say, of course, Sister. But she appears to have been stabbed."

"Oh. Oh, thank you." Death by stabbing could be very swift. "Thank you," the nun said again.

"Yes. Well. Suppose we trade places, Ted. This end of the cart will have to be lifted very high to keep it horizontal. If you'll excuse us, Sister."

Mr. Waddy gave a small bow and set his good gray hat on his curls. He couldn't very well put all his strength into the job of carrying and be hanging on to his hat at the same time.

The young man threw open the door to the stairs. The areaway was enclosed at the top and bottom, and the air of it even in summer was tomblike. No one had considered lighting it. The economical twilight of the hall and the glimmer from the alley above were supposedly enough for a stairs not commonly used. It was startling, then, to meet a pair of eyes gleaming green in the darkness at the top.

"A cat," Mr. Waddy said quietly. "I must have neglected to pull the door shut when we came in. See, it's gone now."

Walking carefully backward, he started up the steps.

The nun did not wait to watch that cautious exit. She did not even turn back to the elevator. She threaded the old labyrinth of halls, hurried up the stairs to the emergency entrance and out into the night. It was very dark. The alley was well populated with cats, she reminded herself. Every moving shadow need not be the murderer.

It was only a short run across the avenue to the convent. The old Octagon House was a landmark built in the heyday of the lumber barons and it had been cut up into rooms oddly shaped because of its eight sides, a make-do convent with inconvenient plumbing and almost no closets. But to Sister Simon it was the most blessed shelter in the world tonight. Up the steps she fled, not pausing until she was inside the screened porch where the lumberman used to stand waving tipsy good-byes to his guests at about this hour of the morning. Nothing had chased her nor even frightened her. On into the house she went, through the central lobby where the circular staircase wound clear up into the cupola, and paused before a solid door marked with a white cross. Behind this door, in the cloister, she had always found peace. The small cares of daily existence had peered through at her, sometimes even made grotesque faces, but she had always been able to push them back across the threshold.

The door must close upon her burdens tonight. She could not bear them longer.

Dipping her finger in the holy-water container, she made the sign of the cross. Then she went inside and shut the door.

Chapter Six

MR. WADDY had not gone home. The early morning sunlight, falling through the Venetian blinds of his office, laid neat slats across the tapestried wall and across Mr. Waddy himself on the davenport. When a slat touched his face he opened his eyes, blinked, and crooked an arm up to shut away the light. It was a little hard for him to tell whether he had been asleep. He did not feel either drowsy or rested. And what he remembered of the night was certainly not a dream.

Shading his eyes with his hand, he looked across the room to the clock on the desk. Six o'clock. It wasn't too early to make the phone call. Vince was an early riser. Mr. Waddy sat up and reached for his high-laced shoes. Not for years had he spent a night at the mortuary. Mrs. Waddy had been somewhat difficult to convince that there was a real need for him to remain here, but in the lethargy of two o'clock in the morning she had been unable to produce much argument. He hadn't known himself exactly why he felt he should stay. Only seeing Dannie again . . . and like that. . . . .

He tied the shoelace into a bowknot, pulling at the loops until they were precisely the same size. Then, dangling the other shoe, he looked up and around the room. He had chosen every detail so carefully. The wallpaper was like woven grass, softly green and tan, the tapestry of ladies and prancing white horses was a museum piece. The carpet was a lovely continuation of shaded green, and against it the cherry-colored chairs and the mahogany desk were richly set off. A far cry, all of it, from the bare room in the back of the furniture store where he had started his undertaking business. The preparation table then had been a storm door laid on sawhorses, the caskets nothing more than grim black boxes. And he had so little in the way of supplies to make a dead person look presentable, especially one who had died in a fire. . . .

Mist swam between Mr. Waddy and the cherry-colored chairs. Fumbling with his other shoe, he pulled out the laces and had to wipe his eyes with the back of his hand before he could see to thread them in again. He was feeling seedy after sleeping in his clothes. He'd get his face washed, then he'd brighten up.

When Mr. Waddy came out of the lavatory off the office, his hair was combed and his glasses polished. There was even an imitation of his customary briskness in the way he slipped on his coat and snapped shut the Venetian blinds to keep out the heat. His hand was on the telephone when a light knock came at the door.

"Come in," Mr. Waddy said.

A tall, very bald man let himself in and closed the door behind him.

"You're early, Snodgrass."

"Yes, sir. I saw the morning paper. The minute I read about it, I knew it was she!" The man came across to the desk with a lithe step. He leaned so close that Mr. Waddy could catch the scent of shaving lotion on his smooth cheeks. "She was *here*, sir! Last night. She asked for you."

The old gentleman laid his hand on his watch chain. He felt as if he were going down very fast in an elevator.

"Why wasn't I summoned, Snodgrass?"

"You had just left for the country."

Mr. Waddy's eyes fell to the desk, to the picture of the grandchildren under the plate glass. Almost any evening of the whole year he would have been available.

"Tell me about her, John."

"That was all, Mr. Waddy. When I said you weren't here she seemed terribly disappointed. She wanted to wait. But I knew you'd stop off at home, just as you did, sir, and I told her that. Didn't I do right?"

"What else could you have done?"

"But she was so frightened, Mr. Waddy, scared to death! She wouldn't even tell me her name!" The man's voice rose. "I feel now as if I — my goodness — I should have put her on a slab if I had to, just to keep her here!"

Mr. Waddy cleared his throat. Snodgrass' finger tips, pressed on the desk, showed nails freshly bitten to the quick.

The role of comforter had never been difficult for Henry Waddy; but now, perhaps because he needed comfort himself, he could find none to pass on. He took Snodgrass by the arm. The arm was tense. All Mr. Waddy could do was to pat it. His voice was gone. Snodgrass had been with him a long time — but not long enough to have known Dannie.

"Go down and make us some coffee, John," Mr. Waddy said when he could speak. Snodgrass' coffee was like seepage from a swamp but it would be a distraction. "Go on. I'll be down as soon as I water the cactus."

The man left. Picking up the telephone, Mr. Waddy dialed.

"Vince? Henry. Could you come over?"

"Yes. Dannie, isn't it?"

"How did you know?"

"Radio."

The line went dead. That was Vince, no waste of words. Mr.

Waddy went into the lavatory, ran a cup half full of water, and spilled it on the cactus as he did every morning. Then, setting the door ajar behind him, he went out of the office.

The hall was still shadowy. Up a couple of steps was the general office, down a few was another door opening off a small landing. Mr. Waddy glanced toward neither. Close to the railing side, he proceeded down the stairs.

More than once in the past Mr. Waddy had come into the airiness of the entrance hall and felt a definite lifting of spirits. On the bottom step he paused, hoping for the lift to come. Trying to help it along, he reviewed how well he had done with transforming the old house. The wide archway made only a gesture of separating the hall from the drawing-room chapel, giving spaciousness to both. Mr. Waddy never had cared about pews. Folding chairs sufficed for funerals and between times, as at present, they could disappear, restoring the pleasant living-room atmosphere. The only feature not commonly found in living rooms was a large recess in the wall opposite the archway. Now the recess held a coffee table upon which stood a pink cyclamen in full bloom. The soft pinks and grays were repeated in the upholstered chairs, davenports, drapes, and carpet, a gently cheering combination. . . .

Abruptly Mr. Waddy's head turned toward the narrow hall leading off the lobby. The workrooms were back there. Some too discreet sound had caught his attention.

"Snodgrass? Is that you?"

But not even Snodgrass' version of coffee could be ready yet. And Ted wouldn't be up. Once, long ago, the boys had left the rear door unlocked and a tramp had wandered in. Mr. Waddy started to investigate. The small corridor was so dark that he was well in before he recognized his visitor.

"Oh," he said. "Vince. Well. I didn't think you could get here so soon."

It almost seemed, from his position, that Vince had just come out of the preparation room. Mr. Waddy knew better than to inquire.

"I hope I didn't phone you too early."

"No."

Vince always talked that way, as if he hated people. And mostly he did. Henry Waddy was about his only friend. The fellow belonged in the woods, really. Tall and gaunt as a Norway pine, he looked like a lumberjack in the plaid shirt and heavy boots he always wore. You'd never take him for a millionaire. Although there was no big timber left in these days, nothing but pulpwood, still he kept to the woods.

Perhaps, Mr. Waddy decided, it would be best to disregard the possibility that Vince had already been in the preparation room.

"I want you to see her, Vince," he said. "If you'll step aside — yes. Thank you."

Together they entered the room, white and clean as a surgery. The one window had a beveled pane with a rim of blue stained glass, and the sun laid a blue rectangle on the gray terrazzo floor. Mr. Waddy opened his cooler and wheeled out a white-sheeted stretcher, pushing and pulling until he had it exactly right. Slowly he lifted the hem of the sheet, folded it back and down until the small face was uncovered. Part of the blue line of light lay around the face like a frame.

Vince drew an audible breath. Considerately, Mr. Waddy did not look at him. But he did note that Vince's horny hands made lumps in his pockets like knots on an oak tree.

"I hadn't seen her for years," Mr. Waddy said. "She came here last night, asking for me. I was out. Would you have any idea what she wanted, Vince?"

"No."

"You hadn't talked with her lately?"

"No."

Mr. Waddy's glance flicked his friend. The bony jaw was dark and unshaven, the muscles tight.

"She reminds me of Elizabeth," Mr. Waddy said.

"Elizabeth McArthur's dead twenty years."

In a near room a radio blasted on and was immediately quieted to a drumbeat. Mr. Waddy cocked his head in the listening attitude that had become a mannerism.

"Yes. Well. Twenty years is nearly a generation, isn't it?"

"If you mean the girl, Diane, she's grown up."

"I was thinking of Elizabeth."

Vince finally looked at him, and Mr. Waddy continued. "She was the first one I used the wax on. She wasn't too badly burned, considering she was in the house when it went. But I couldn't have let anyone see her without the wax. One of the nuns — can you think of her name, Vince, a strapping big woman — she said I'd made her natural as life."

He paused, but Vince made no reply. "We still use the wax in the same way, only now we rebuild features mostly after auto accidents. It's very soft, to prevent cracking, and people are sometimes curious, they want to touch a face, and fingers leave dents. So we drape the veil of net from the lid of the casket out over — "

Vince wheeled. Before he could reach the door, the old gentleman's quiet voice stopped him.

"You understand my code of ethics, Vince. I never volunteer information. If the police want to get something out of me they have to obtain a court order to do it. Not that I wish to place obstacles in their way but I feel very strongly . . ."

"You've told me before, Henry."

"I feel very strongly that a funeral director must never be connected with anything in the least sensational. It would be

bad, very bad for my name to be linked with this case in any way." Again Mr. Waddy paused. "There may be no reason, of course, to dig into the past."

"Can't we wait and see?"

"Certainly."

There was a ragged look about Vince that Mr. Waddy couldn't bear. "I'll see that she has a nice funeral. I can't exclude the thrill seekers, I'm afraid, for the manner of her death invites them, but I'll make sure that there is no disrespect. . . ."

No point in continuing. Vince had charged out into the hall as if the whole place were crammed with underbrush to be trampled down. Mr. Waddy cocked his head, listening. You couldn't exactly say that Vince slammed the door, but you did know unmistakably that he had gone out.

Mr. Waddy drew a deep breath. He must not keep Dannie out here in the warmth too long. The sun had moved, laying the blue frame a little closer about her face. Women always fascinated him from the time they attained the use of reason at the approximate age of three until they were carried in through his back door. You'd almost swear that some of them, during their last seconds of life, had stood before the pearly gates and seen inside. The men, judging from their expressions, might have gone anywhere. The women made you believe in heaven.

"Yes. Well," Mr. Waddy said aloud.

With a delicate sort of tenderness the old gentleman laid the sheet back in place. If the call hadn't come to take him away last night, if he had been able to talk with Dannie — but why go over it in vain regretting? Vince was the one to think of now.

Chapter Seven

LIZETTE sat in the second chair in the third row and stared at the blackboard. This was the room in which the nurses' aides had their classes, and someone with a flair for slogans had written on the board, "Carefulness, Cleanliness, Courtesy." The word "Courtesy" sat neatly on Chief Wakeley's shoulder as he stood at the desk, talking. Seated at the desk was a young policeman who wrote earnestly in a notebook and never seemed to get caught up because his pencil always went on writing through the pauses. Not that there had been many pauses. The questions had come rapidly. Everyone was assembled who could conceivably know the slightest detail about the little woman's visit to the hospital and her subsequent death — even Diane, who hadn't had to come. Right up to the door of the room Lizette had heard Mother Richard explaining to her that she need not be questioned with the others, the Chief had said so. But Diane insisted on hearing everything for herself. And now she sat in the chair ahead of Lizette with Mother Richard beside her. Over at the end of the row, nearest the door, was another nun, Sister Simon. Lizette had glanced at her but once. She had very raw feelings concerning Sister Simon.

Since eight o'clock — it was nine now — the Chief had been digging away at the scant information the hospital staff could give him. He had the look about him of a very determined woodpecker, probably because he combed his black hair back in a shining crest. His shoulders were even wider than Ted's and he had a way of pushing his chin forward as if he were literally uprooting facts. It could be, Lizette reflected, that his collar was too tight; but the gesture gave him an air of stern tenacity. And stubbornness. You probably couldn't change his mind about anything. For instance, about the picture he was building up of Dannie Grear. Like any tourist, he said, she came to town and went sight-seeing down on the water front.

"She arrived by bus, we know that," he said, although he had gone over all this before. He turned to Lizette. "Judging from the time you saw her, Miss Carter, she must have gone straight down to the river. Apparently she was under your observation the entire time she was there. You say she spoke to no one, not even to you. Isn't that the normal conduct of a person among strangers?"

"Yes, sir. But she was afraid," Lizette said. She had said it before. She could be stubborn, too, particularly when she was telling the truth.

"Did you see anyone or anything to frighten you?"

"No, sir."

"According to her niece, Miss Grear had no enemies."

"Of course she hadn't!" Diane broke in. "She was a wonderful person! Everybody loved her. Think of what she did for me, raising me after my mother died in the fire! Why, she was the dearest, sweetest . . . "

The girl's voice broke, and Lizette leaned forward to lay a hand on her shoulder. "Diane, I know! I only meant that somebody . . . "

"Mr. Peters said she was the best clerk he ever had, too. And she was with him twenty years! She brought all kinds of customers to the store!"

Mother Richard whispered something, and Diane subsided.

"We've pretty well established the kind of person she was," Wakeley said. "Let's return to the facts. She did have a suitcase when you saw her on the water front, Miss Carter? You're sure of that?"

"Yes, sir, the paper kind that looks like tweed. They're not very expensive."

"And a purse?"

"Yes."

"Now Miss Barlow." He faced Evvie. "You saw that she had the purse when she came in here to the desk?"

"Sure, I told you about it. Black. But she didn't have the suitcase. I'd of noticed."

"She could have left it in the waiting room, couldn't she, without you knowing?"

"Well — I guess so."

"But when you found her, Miss Carter, you didn't see the purse or the suitcase anywhere around?"

"I didn't look," Lizette said shortly.

Mother Richard's veil made a small motion of annoyance. She expected her people to co-operate fully with the police. She had made a few remarks on the subject, precisely and formally, before Wakeley came in.

"She was scared, all right," Evvie said suddenly. "I could tell."

"How could you tell?"

Good for you, Evvie, now don't back down, Lizette urged silently. But Evvie, confronted by a situation which called for brainwork, was at a loss.

"Well, I just knew. Like I know I'm scared now!"

There was a rustle of laughter and people shifting in their chairs. Wakeley even smiled, a rugged, he-man smile that put women and their intuition in their proper place. Lizette fixed her gaze upon Mrs. Van Courtland, the life-size dummy whom the nurses' aides had tucked up primly in her hospital bed. It would be very handy to be like Mrs. Van Courtland, no feelings about anything.

"You are probably right, Miss Barlow," the Chief said. "She was scared because she knew she had been followed out here. Somebody, seeing her down on the water front, decided she had some money. So he followed her, hung around outside while she was in here, and when she came out again he struck. The purse and the suitcase are both missing." His chin prodded forward again. "But we'll find them, and we'll find who killed her. It may take time but we'll do it. That's all for now, ladies and gentlemen, and thank you for your patience. If you remember anything more, no matter how small, call my office."

Everyone stood up, talking with conscious ease, and began to move out of the room. Lizette walked to the back windows. She was not going to face Sister Simon. The room grew silent, the voices became a disappearing drone in the hall. She turned, and discovered that she was alone with Sister Simon.

The nun looked as if she had not slept at all. She was beside a chair, holding on to the back as if she actually needed the support.

"I've taken you off duty for tonight, Lizette," she said. "Virginia needs to get in some extra hours."

"Thank you, Sister. But I'd rather work."

A faint flush rose in the Sister's cheeks. Lizette added coldly, "You need not upset your schedule, Sister. Rules are so important."

"My duty last night was to my patients, not to a strange woman who had no claim on us. You should understand that, Lizette."

"Oh, I do! But isn't it a little rough on people who need help and can find nobody in the world with time to help them?"

The nun bit her lip but even then it trembled. Lizette looked away. She was going to cherish the resentment she felt against everyone who refused to see into Dannie Grear's tragedy, and everyone included Sister Simon.

"She asked for Diane, Evvie said," Lizette went on, addressing a chart showing the complete digestive system. "When Diane wasn't in, then she thought of me. Not because she knew me well — we'd only met once at a tea — but because she had to have someone to be with *then!* Not an hour and a half later, when Diane would be home, but right that minute! She didn't want to be alone because she was *afraid for her life!*"

To her dismay, Lizette felt a tear start down her cheek. Slapping it away, she cut through a row of chairs to the door.

"But don't let it bother you, Sister," she said in the doorway. "You did the right thing."

Then she ran because she knew she was going to cry and cry and cry.

Sister Simon stood for a long minute hanging on to the chair back. She *had* done the right thing. Lizette was heartbroken now over her memory of the woman's suffering. In her replies to the police officer's questions, her remorse had been evident. She was scourging herself because she had not helped the woman when she met her on the water front, and anyone who touched upon the incident would be scourged also. The girl's resentment was understandable. And perhaps there *might* have been a way out. . . .

Sister Simon left the room, walked down the two flights of stairs to the emergency entrance and out into the alley. Mother Richard could still be with Diane; but also she could be in the spot she always said was her choice, next to the chapel, for meditation. Crossing the avenue and skirting around the old

Octagon House, Sister Simon went quickly out through the vacant lots toward the bluff.

She could see from a distance that Mother Richard was on her knees in the vegetable garden. No other nun wore the same kind of striped apron. She had pinned back her sleeves and her veil and she was breaking over onion tops. A few rows away Sister Joe was working. The old nun was so deaf that her presence would not hinder a private conversation.

Sister Simon halted between the rows. The pungent odor of the crushed greens and the perfume drawn out of the clover by the hot sun was as homely a mingling as one could imagine. Impossible to relate onion juice and murder.

Mother Richard sat back on her heels. She was not wearing gloves and the pulp stained her hands. She rested them, palm up, on her knees. Her age was right to make her the mother of the younger nuns. The smile failed to put the customary twinkle in her eyes.

"Have you come to help pull the radishes, Sister? They're going to seed."

Sister Simon tried to return the smile. The attempt was a sorry affair. Better to gaze out over the river. The bluff where she stood was a lofty lookout, affording a panoramic view of the far bank. Over there, a few miles back from the shore line, the glacier of an ancient age had crept to a halt and its melting torrents had cut chasms down through rock layers so deep that a person exploring them on a summer day would shiver in the moist twilight, and so narrow that he would have to turn sideways to pass through. Small creeks now trickled down the beds worn by those mad, whirling streams. A man could hide there for weeks, undiscovered — a murderer. Her father had been killed by a murderer he and another policeman were trying to apprehend, and she had promised herself then and there that she would become a detective and avenge all murders. At thirteen, there had been nothing impossible about that. Her father had taught her to shoot "from the hip," that is, without using the sights. She could hit a moving target at fifty feet with a pistol — a skill you seldom needed in the convent. She still could do it, as she had proved at the last nurses' picnic. . . .

"What is troubling you, Sister?" Mother Richard asked, getting to her feet. She was short and portly, a comfortable housewife of the Middle Ages in the ancient dress. Behind her, in spirit, were ranged all the thousands of women who had worn the habit and kept the rule, losing the world to gain heaven.

Sister Simon bent and pulled off a sprig of radish blossom.

"Mother — duty has nothing to do with sentiment, has it? Duty is assigned, a law requiring administration on the one hand and obedience on the other. Because I'm a supervisor, I'm an administrator. But I still have the obligation of being obedient to the law myself. I must not set it aside for personal considerations. Am I right, Mother?"

"Of course."

"Then . . ." The radish flower slid down against her apron. "Then why am I in such a state of confusion?"

"All this has something to do with last night, Sister?"

"Yes, Mother. The woman — Dannie Grear — had Everine call up to the floor for Lizette. I told the police officer about it. He thought nothing of it, as evidence."

"I remember. You had an emergency at about the same time."

"A few minutes later. But not just then. Mother, I could have let Lizette go down!"

Mother Richard stepped over the onions. Taking the Sister's left hand, she spread her own pudgy, freckled left hand beside it. Each wore a plain silver band.

"We both wear the ring, Sister," she said, pushing her thumb up against her own. "See how tight mine has become? I doubt if I could get it off now. It's made a groove for itself right in my flesh. Forty years deep. Yours is still loose, you see." She patted the hand. "We wear the ring because we chose it, Sister. Nobody made us do so; we entered the convent of our own free will. While I was a novice I had long talks with Sister Joseph, she was Mother Superior then — the same kind of talks you had with me. You understood before you took your vows that the life of the convent is all according to rule, right down to the smallest detail. A bell rings and we obey, our superior speaks and we obey without question. We agree to live by the rule, that's our way of life." Mother patted the hand again and released it. "Don't worry about your doubts, Sister, just dismiss them. By the time your fingers are as fat as mine you'll have no doubts any more."

Sister Simon smiled faintly. "That will be a happy day, Mother."

"You did the right thing last night, Sister. The woman's death is tragic but it had nothing to do with you. Forget about it as best you can."

"Yes, Mother. Thank you."

Pondering the simplicity of Mother Richard's wisdom, the nun started back along the path. Sister Joseph was ahead of her, trudging with a pail of beets. She caught up to the old Sister and stepped out to pass her.

Sister Joe nodded a greeting. Her wrinkled face was browned to the hue of an Indian in sharp contrast to the white coif.

"There seems to be excitement in the air this morning, Sister," she boomed. Her tone was loud because she could barely hear herself.

Sister Simon beckoned for the pad of paper and the pencil the old nun always carried in her pocket.

"A woman died last night. At the hospital," she wrote. Then for no obvious reason, she added the name, "Dannie Grear."

Sister Joe read and reread the message. "Some doctor's carelessness?" she asked finally.

In haste, Sister Simon wrote, "Murder," and handed back the pencil. It was pathetic, she thought as she hurried on, that Sister Joe must depend on someone's whim to hear the news. She must pay more attention herself and she would remind the others.

But she didn't think long about the old nun. She had been gone too long from the floor and her work was waiting. She knew now what to say to Lizette, and she would say it at the first opportunity. She could make Lizette understand.

In the hospital corridors Lizette had managed to elude everyone who might ask questions; but when she sped across the alley and yanked open the door to the nurses' home, she was afraid her luck was ended. The very air was vibrant with the hum of voices. Even the kids who had come off night duty must be chattering away. And there would be only one subject. The murder. How would she ever get past all those open doors to the telephone? Someone did call out, but Lizette pretended not to hear as she ran by.

Mr. Waddy answered her telephone call. He said that Ted had gone out.

"He isn't there? Where did he go?" Lizette asked childishly.

That, she knew, was silly. Mr. Waddy would have no idea of what his boys did in their free time. He told her so, kindly.

"Thank you," Lizette said, ". . . No, no message."

What message could she leave — that the bottom had fallen out of the morning, that she had become such a clinging vine as to feel all uprooted when she couldn't find Ted?

"Here, kitty, here's your breakfast, come kitty-kitty-kitty!" a girl called over by the alley door.

Antonia was putting out scraps for Liz's dependents, as they called the cats. The kids would all be good. But thoughtless. They would want a million details.

"Hi. I thought I saw you flit by my door. Without so much as a good morning, either."

Lizette looked up wearily. Sybil, as usual, was barefooted. But her red hair was brushed into coppery highlights and her silver-flowered housecoat was the kind most of the girls would only sigh over in a store window.

"I shouldn't even tell you what I'm supposed to tell you," she remarked, draping herself against the wall. Sybil always moved as if a gallery of eligible males were watching. "But I'm a superior-type maiden. I won't even make you suffer." Her green eyes came languidly to Lizette. "Boy, do you look shot!"

"What are you supposed to tell me?"

"Your boy friend's waiting for you in the mush room."

"Not Ted?"

"None other than. I was going to hold back until you'd given me a firsthand account of finding the corpse, because I knew you'd dash off — sure, there you go."

"Well, get me some clothes, then. I'll dress in the shower room and give you a blow-by-blow description."

"Goody. What do you want to put on?"

"Shorts. The white ones. And borrow a blouse from Jinny."

"Our little Jinny, what would we do without her."

"And tell Ted I'll be right there."

"I'll tell him that in the course of human events you'll show up. You owe me a decent minute, dearie."

Sybil drifted away and Lizette ran for the shower room.

Ten minutes later she entered the violet parlor. Ted, relaxing on his spine in a lavender chair, removed his gaze from the painting of a white madonna with purple pansies which took up the space above the violet love seat.

"Hello, hon. I was just sitting here wondering who decorated this cheery little spot, anyway."

"For goodness' sake, does it matter? Ted, Dannie Grear was mur . . ."

"Any guy with dishonorable intentions would sure feel he was getting the cold shoulder." Ted pulled himself out of the chair. "Old Waddy never uses purple — too chilly."

"Ted, aren't you even interested in . . ."

"I'm interested in you, punkin. And I want you to stay in low gear. I'm going to take you on a picnic."

"Are you really? Up the Gorge?"

"Absolutely." He kissed her on the forehead. "See, out of deference to the saintly nun who put her all into this room, I won't even kiss you here. But out in the primitive wilds — aha!"

He picked up the large paper sack from the floor beside his chair. Lizette laughed shakily. Ted always did that to her, made her feel cared for and carefree. It was perfectly possible that he wouldn't let her mention the murder at all.

Eddie was skulking, not walking, up the narrow sidewalk that threaded the Witches' Gorge. Knees slightly bent, putting your heel down first and rolling, sort of, on to your toe, that was how you skulked. Eddie knew because he had seen Indians doing it on television. He was not an Indian this morning, though, he was a sheriff's scout. A band of outlaws had held up the stagecoach right out in the oak grove behind the barn and he had seen the whole thing while he was gathering eggs in the henhouse. He had sneaked off as soon as he could make it, trailing the gang cross-country to the Gorge. It wasn't far from home, exactly, but you could make it seem farther if you took it easy and doubled back quite a bit. His mother never wanted him to come over here — letting the kid run wild, she called it — but his dad couldn't see anything wrong with it, provided he got his chores done first. Mom wouldn't fuss today. She was too busy making little sandwiches for her bridge club this afternoon, and she'd want him out of the way anyhow. Eddie hated the bridge club. The ladies all acted as if they were going to pat him on the head, and somebody would always ask how old he was. Next time he wasn't going to say eight, he'd say about forty-seven and maybe they'd quit. . . .

He stopped, stock still. High up on the rock wall there was a scrambling sound, too small for a bandit but enough to let Eddie bring the gun up in position against his shoulder. Sighting along the barrel, he looked smack into the face of an astonished chipmunk. The chipmunks didn't often come down here, too dark and damp.

"Bang!" he said.

The chipmunk flicked its tail. Eddie swung the muzzle up, sighting for more game. The Gorge was deep as a house, the sky a narrow blue ribbon running along up there with ferns and things hanging over from the forest floor. The walls were of cross-bedded rock, smooth sometimes, then again stacked up like a giant's dinner plates with moss in patches as if the giant's wife hadn't scraped the plates very clean. Down here where the sidewalk was, nothing lived, not even snakes. But from about half past two in the afternoon until dark there would be tourists tramping through here led by a guide in a blue uniform. That was why the boat company had built the sidewalk, so the people could walk along and not get their feet wet. Eddie dropped to his stomach and peered over the edge of the planks. The creek was still there, all right. But little, like somebody farther up was maybe just dumping out their canteen. It sure sounded like a tall story that about a billion trillion years ago the creek was a great big river tearing through the rocks, running down from the glacier when it melted. He wouldn't believe all that, only his dad had told it. The water had whirled so hard it had scooped regular little round rooms out under the dinner plates. Some of the rooms were plenty big so a bandit could get in there and hide if he wanted to. A dandy place to cache the loot from the stagecoach, too.

Eddie laid the gun carefully on the sidewalk. His hands were all rusty from it, but that didn't matter. He'd wash them good in the chickens' drinking trough when he got home. It was possible that his mother wouldn't take the gun away from him even if she discovered it, but there was no sense taking chances. The skulking had sure been more fun since he'd found the shootin' iron in the river. That was another reason for not letting Mom know about the gun. She'd said not to go near the river.

Sliding between the boards of the guard rail, Eddie hooked his bare toes into the cracked rock that was the threshold of the room. The rock was awfully cold. Even a stagecoach robber would have to be pretty desperate to hide in here very long. He peered back into the dimness. Maybe there weren't any snakes in the Gorge, but it sure looked like there ought to be. Or lizards. Something tiny moved, away in the back.

Eddie scuttled out so fast, backward, that he slipped under the sidewalk, caught at the planks, ran a long sliver into his thumb, got himself mostly soaked in the creek, and finally swung in under the guard rail. Grabbing the gun, he streaked up the Gorge. Wet like this, he was cold. In his den the sun would be hot and he'd be dry in no time.

He was breathing hard when he reached the Witches' Glen at the head of the Gorge. It was big as a living room, overgrown with scrubby trees and ferns, and partly roofed by the cross-bedded rock. He could sun himself here, but the den would be even better. Jumping to a rounded rock, then to the next, he used the left foot first. He always did it that way because the left foot never got to be first and it deserved some turns, too. Part way up the side Eddie paused, looked around for enemies, and then slipped between the vertical layers of a rock wall.

The chamber he entered was open to the sky but sunken to the depth of a room below the forest floor. The rock ledges were padded with moss and vines, and tall trees threw shade from the plateau. Eddie had always known — about two weeks — that someone else used the den, too, because the ashes of the campfire in the middle of the rock floor were sometimes different. But he never had met the other user. Now he did. A girl, down on her knees beside the fire, was frying bacon in a black old pan, and she had a pot of coffee bubbling so hard it made little spittings out through the spout. She was alone now, but she probably wouldn't be for long because two paper plates were set side by side on a ledge, and there were two forks.

She didn't seem a bit surprised to see a visitor. She was pretty, like his teacher last year. Sitting back on her heels, she smiled. She was even prettier then.

"Hi," she said. "Had your breakfast?"

Eddie scowled. He liked the girl already, but none of the strong men in the TV westerns got friendly right off the bat.

"Where's he?" he asked. She did look surprised, then, so he pointed the gun at the paper plates. "Him. You got two."

"Say, that's pretty sharp of you. He's up there getting more wood."

She waved the fork toward the plateau, then began to nip the bacon out of the pan and drop it on a paper napkin.

"Have a bite with us? I'll put in an extra egg."

"Oh. . . . I dunno."

"As long as we use your hide-out, we'd better be buddies."

"O.K." Eddie watched the eggs bubble up in white blisters. "How'd you know this was my hide-out?"

"Well, once I left the frying pan right side up in the pantry over there, and when I came to get it next time, it was the way it ought to be, bottom up. Nobody but a real woodsman would have bothered about that."

Eddie scowled hard at the rocky recess she called the pantry. He remembered very well how he had taken everything out and examined it. Putting the frying pan back as she said was pure accident.

"I figured you'd forgot," he muttered. "You gotta be careful with frying pans."

"Sure, they rust," she said as if Eddie knew all about it; so he nodded as if he did.

There was quite a crackling now up on the plateau and a tall young man appeared.

"Timber-r-r!" he called, and dropped down his armful of wood before he came skidding after it. "Hi, fella," he grinned at Eddie.

"This is Ted," the girl said. "I'm Lizette. He's a guide for the boat company."

"I seen you yesterday comin' up the draw," Eddie told the young man. "I seen you lots of times, two maybe."

"I bring settlers in regular."

"You never even knew I was there, did you?"

"No, siree, you're a pretty smooth scout, good as Jim Bowie."

"You and Jim Bowie could dig into the buffalo steak if we had another plate," Lizette said. "And a cup. I'll give him a little coffee."

"She makes the finest coffee this side of the Pecos, Jim," Ted declared, winking. "Pure smoke and ashes." He reached into the pantry right from where he sat, his arms were that long.

Eddie couldn't get over it, the way they fell into playing the game without any questions. The girl portioned out the eggs and bacon and a piece of bread and handed a plate to him. It smelled wonderful, just as you'd imagine when you'd see the campfires leaping on TV.

Eddie laid aside his gun to take the plate.

"Dandy shootin' iron you got there," Ted remarked. "Put up much gold for it?"

"Didn't cost me nothin'. I hooked it in the river, fishin'."

"Whadda ya know! Hand it over a minute."

Eating with one hand, Ted examined the gun, even sighted along the rusty old barrel. He wouldn't have to be told that the working parts didn't work.

"I bet it's great for antelope, eh, Jim?"

"I ain't brought down much with it yet, just a few chipmunks."

"How do you suppose it got into the river, Ted?" Lizette asked.

"Hard to tell. Somebody was deer hunting and lost it, maybe. Could have been crossing the river and his boat upset." He ran his thumb over the wooden stock. "He cut his initials here. W something."

"W L," Eddie said. "I washed it off good in the chickens' trough. You could see it plain when it was wet."

"Too bad it isn't W E," said Lizette. "Then it would be Wyatt Earp."

Ted seemed to consider this seriously. He even put down his bread so he could study the lettering better. Eddie held his breath.

"It *is* W E, dogged if it ain't!" Ted exclaimed. "Funny I didn't notice it!"

Eddie scrambled over on his knees until he was hard against Ted's shoulder. "Where? Where's the E?"

"Right there, bright as day, only you can't make out the arms of the E because the waves wore them down till you'd swear it's an L. Looky here, I'll get out my knife. . . ."

"Your Bowie knife," Lizette corrected.

"Sure thing. And I'll carve that E out real fine."

"But eat your pemmican first," Lizette reminded him. "You have to keep up your strength, you and Jim."

"Absolutely. To the feed bag, Jim!"

"And don't gobble. I'm going to have a nap here in the shade so you'll have time to carve the whole alphabet if you're a mind to."

"Women," Ted said, and winked broadly.

Eddie crawled back to his plate. He was so excited he felt like the balloons down at the river park, light and dancing. He hadn't had such a great time all summer.

Sister Joseph was sorely perplexed. She didn't have the slightest idea of what to do about the letter. She sat in her rocker and leaned forward with her elbows on her knees, the letter in her hand, her brooding gaze on the contents of the box on the floor before her. It was an apple box she had covered, lid and all, with calico years before and it still was a good box. It contained her treasures: a scrapbook, a chipped statue of the Blessed Mother, old rosaries, papers, a piece of crocheting, and a deck of cards. With the lid down, and under her bed, the box was as safe a place as one could wish for. No one ever touched another's possessions in the cloister. But put the letter in there and every time she came to the box she would see it. No, definitely this letter must go into the book. Her old face took on a softening of relief. Laying the lid in place, she pushed the box back under the bed. She saw that the Japanese glass chimes on her bookcase swayed and touched as she tramped across to the closet. It would be nice to hear the chimes. But at least she could see well. And the crown of her head still touched the six-foot-one mark made on the kitchen door by the novices so long ago.

Pushing back the curtain which shut away her closet, Sister Joe reached easily to the top shelf. Two books? Hadn't she always had but one up here? *Muskox, Bison, Sheep, and Goats,* by Caspar Whitney and Others. That was the old stand-by, the best book she had ever had for forgetting. She frowned at the other, bound in brisk new red: *Uranium Prospecting in Northern Minnesota.*

"Of course," she said. She knew she spoke aloud because she felt the vibration in her throat. She did remember now about the uranium book. She had picked it up in a room the nurses' aides were cleaning and the aides had said, every last one of them, that she should keep it. A book you never read is an excellent place to tuck away a letter you'd like to forget about. Mr. Whitney's volume had been entrusted with enough secrets through the years so that they were likely to fall out, which was disastrous to forgetting. She really needed this second book.

She flipped through the new pages. She had put nothing at all in it yet. A perfect hiding place for Damian's letter. Sister Joe laid the envelope between the pages and closed the book tightly. But then she hesitated. Was it right just to forget what Damian had said? Not said, exactly, but certainly hinted. I'm going to talk it all over with you, that was what she had put in the letter. But she hadn't said when the talk would be.

It would be never, now. Sister Simon had said that Damian was dead. And since death had ended the long tragedy, surely it was best to forget about the letter. Stretching up, Sister Joe pushed the book far back on the shelf. Then she looked at her clock. At ten, she would go to the kitchen to slip the skins off the beets for Sister Mary Clement. She had fifteen minutes. Seating herself again in the rocker, she pulled out the apple box and carefully extracted the scrapbook. Niagara Falls, on the cover, was faded until it looked like a wheatfield after a hailstorm. She laid open the book across her knees, turning the pages cautiously. They were broken around the edges and tiny bits fell in chaff down her scapular. Photographs, name's day cards, and little notes of spiritual bouquets she turned past, page after page.

"Ah," she said aloud.

The page under her hand was pasted full of newspaper clippings on which the glue showed through in brown patches. But the print was readable. "Hunter Accidentally Shot in Cabin, Brother Missing." With what impact that headline had hit the convent on the morning it came out!

Propping the book against the bed, she turned the page. On the back she had pasted something of less importance. In fact, she couldn't remember now why she had saved it at all. "Third Hunter Lost in Woods." She read the first line. "The sheriff's office reported this morning that Willis Lawrence of Beechwood Falls failed to rejoin his party. . . ."

Her attention wandered. A man named Willis Lawrence could have nothing to do with Damian. Turning back to the first page, she began to read. Someone else had slipped the skins off the beets before she remembered her duty down in the kitchen.

Chapter Eight

LATE in the afternoon Lizette lay on as much of her bed as Evvie had left to her and did her best to think about nothing. She and Ted had prolonged their picnic until nearly one o'clock, coming back barely in time for him to change into his uniform and make it to the dock for his first boat trip. The pleasant relaxation of the morning still lingered with her. Because of Sybil's foresight, the "Do Not Disturb!" sign on the door was having its effect. On the other bed, Jinny sat crosslegged in her slip, little piles of papers all around her. Sybil, the volunteer guard, was curled up on Jinny's pillows.

"I'm going to poison that lousy ivy," Evvie said. "Hey, you don't care if I use your nail polish, do you, Liz?"

Lizette grunted. She had been smelling the strong banana odor for quite some time.

"What ivy?" she asked.

"You're not supposed to talk to her, Ev," Sybil said. "She's asleep."

"She'd sleep better if you kids got out," Jinny remarked. "I'd be real still. I'm studying."

"What ivy?" Lizette asked again.

"The one over the lobby arch. In the hospital. The way it swings, it gives me the willies."

"Just when the door is open, though," Jinny put in. "That's all it swings."

"Well, sure. But look at last night, the stupid thing swinging away and nobody coming in."

"Couldn't they of gone in the waiting room? You wouldn't see."

"The woman was in the waiting room — oh, glory, it could of been the murd . . ."

The word was cut off as if a hand had been clapped over Evvie's mouth. Sybil's hand, because Jinny took up the idea in a frightened whisper.

"D'you suppose he dragged her outside and plunged a knife in her . . . ?"

"*Jinny!*" Sybil cautioned.

Lizette sat up. Jinny was looking as if she herself had just confronted the murderer face to face, and Evvie had spilled the nail polish in her lap.

"Now look what you made me do!" Evvie squealed, and Sybil snapped, "It was your own fault! Don't move or it'll go all over the bed."

"Like blood," Jinny whispered.

"Jin, I'll choke you yet!" Sybil warned.

But Evvie cut in excitedly. "I don't see why we shouldn't talk! My brother-in-law says Liz is going to be next."

"What does your brother-in-law know about it?"

"Plenty! Gordie says maybe the guy was right down there on the water front when Liz talked to the woman, because that's when she said the woman got so scared, and the cop didn't believe you, Liz, but Gordie does. He says you've sure got good reason to worry!"

"I haven't been worrying."

"Then you better! Because Gordie says you're the only one could really identify him. You looked maybe right *at* him and he knows it!"

"But *I* don't know it. I mean, I have no idea what scared the woman. . . ."

"Sure, but even the cop says it was somebody killed her, who followed her up from the water front and robbed her!"

"Robbery wasn't the motive! How could she be afraid ahead of time of somebody that was going to hold her up?"

"You see?" Evvie declared triumphantly. She leaped up and a sticky puddle of polish streamed to the floor. "See, you talk just like Gordie. He says you better look out. . . ."

"Ev, will you *shut up!*" Sybil commanded. "Get your skirt off, it's ruined anyway, and wipe up this mess."

"Well, it's fair to warn her, and I wouldn't be in her shoes for a million dollars," Evvie muttered, but she stepped out of her skirt and went down on her knees, mopping.

Surprised at herself for trembling, Lizette lay down again. Her own possible danger was something she had not considered. She hadn't seen the person who frightened Dannie Grear, she had told the police so; it would most likely even be in the paper tonight! But the criminal couldn't be sure. The only certain means of preventing identification by her would be to . . .

"The darn stain isn't coming out at all!" Evvie wailed, rubbing at the floor. "What'll I do?"

"Use some polish remover," Sybil retorted in a tone short of patience. "Not Lizette's, either. And get a move on. I've got to wash my hair."

"Well, go ahead. And you don't have to bite my head off! I guess I'm just as good a friend of Liz's as you are, heaps better if I . . . "

"We're all friends," Lizette broke in, "so let's act like it. Going out on a heavy date, Sybil?"

"The only thing heavy about it is the character I'm going with."

"Chuck?"

"Roger. I can't stand him."

"Then why go?" Jinny asked.

"I wouldn't if somebody else . . . Jin! How about you?"

"*Me?*"

"You *must* hate the guy," Evvie remarked, getting up with the skirt wadded in her hand.

"Shut the door as you leave," Sybil suggested.

"Oh, cut it out, kids," Lizette sighed. "Leave us have peace and quiet."

Everine's large dark eyes, so effective with the ash-blond hair, filled with tears. "Liz, you're so good! I just hope nothing — nothing — I mean . . ."

"Farewell, friend," Sybil said, and she marched over and kicked the door shut on the very tail of Evvie's slip.

"Friends are *nice!*" Jinny burst out unexpectedly. "And Evvie has real good common sense. I haven't; Mother Richard says so. I haven't got any judgment at all, except bad. And Evvie's scared, right to the marrow of her bones! That's what friends are for!"

"To scare the liver out of you?" Sybil asked.

"To do things for you. When you're in trouble or in need or something, then your friends help you out. I'd do anything for Liz!"

"How about for me?"

"But that's different! I've never been out with a boy in my life!"

"You handled the queen business last year without breaking a leg, didn't you? So you can muddle through this. And look what's in it for you, a meal that didn't come out of a wash boiler, scintillating conversation with a razor brain."

"I wouldn't know what to talk about."

"Worms," said Sybil, seating herself again on the bed. "He's a biologist. Or dead cats. He's taking anatomy, too."

"Now you're laughing at me! I'm not so dumb I can't tell when you're . . ."

"Jinny, dear," Lizette said, doing her best to remember that patience is a virtue, "honey, why don't you go out with Roger and have a good time? Don't be so tense. You're a sweet child and you have a lot more on the ball than you think. Roger will love you."

"If I could be like you, all poised and everything, I'd go in a minute."

"Forget about poise and you'll have it."

"I haven't got a thing to wear!"

"How about my orchid nylon?" Sybil asked. "You'd look like the Czaress of Timbuktu, with your blond hair."

"You haven't even worn it yet yourself! What if I tear it?"

"Dearie, this is a dinner party, not a wrestling match."

The door burst open and Antonia bounced in.

"Phone for you, Liz."

"Who is it?"

"Your one and only."

"I thought he was on the high seas," Lizette said, but she reached for her housecoat. "Thanks, Tony. Bye bye, kiddies, see you much, much later."

"Aren't you coming back?" Jinny asked.

"She means we won't be here when she gets back," Sybil explained. "O.K., just for that, we'll borrow her shampoo. You can dress in my room, too. Grab the unmentionables and we won't have to bother Miss Exclusive again."

Sybil certainly meant business, Lizette thought as she went down the hall. Sybil never lent her clothes. And never shampooed any hair but her own. She probably had another date up her sleeve for tonight.

"Hi, Ted," Lizette said into the telephone. "What's new?"

"Nothing much. Did I wake you up?"

"In this monkey house? Hardly."

"Going on duty tonight?"

"Of course. At eleven. Why?"

"You'll sleep through the dinner hour?"

"I was planning on it."

"Then I won't come over between trips. I'd like to go back and see what's up with poor old Waddy, anyway. Looks to me like he's in a bad state."

"Sick?"

"Practically. Wanders around like a chicken with its head cut off. He knew Dannie Grear, I told you that."

"I remember."

"I've been wondering if the old guy didn't maybe want to marry her sometime. Before Mrs. Waddy, that is."

"She'd have been too young. He has grown-up sons."

"Yeah, you're right. But he's sure taking it hard. Liz . . ."

"What?"

"Wouldn't you come over and see her? He's done a swell job on her. . . ."

"No. N O."

"Well, have a good sleep."

"I will. Ted . . . I . . . The kids were saying . . . I mean, Evvie thinks . . ."

"Thinks what?"

"Nothing."

"What is it, Liz?"

"Nothing, honestly. Will I see you tomorrow morning?"

"I'll be on the doorstep with the morning paper. Jerry's tooting for me. 'Bye, honey."

Lizette put down the telephone slowly. Ted was not an alarmist — he would never agree with Gordie. And she could hardly be in danger for the next few hours. Let the future take care of itself. She picked up a scrap of chalk and wrote on the blackboard, "No calls. Carter."

When she reached her room the girls were gone. A great deal of chatter issued from Sybil's room down the hall. Lizette shut herself in, pulled down the shade and flopped onto the bed. Almost before she kicked off her slippers, she was sound asleep.

"There's no help for it, Snodgrass," said Mr. Waddy.

Still, he came once again to the door of the small room and looked out across the lobby into the drawing-room chapel.

"No," he said finally, turning back, "no, it's much too public. We couldn't protect her out there. Here we can."

"I feel that this is rather cozy, sir," Snodgrass said, and he tilted his head to one side, a mannerism he had picked up from Mr. Waddy. They had pulled the heavy drapes shut and turned on the ceiling light, and the glare skidded across his bald head. He moved a candelabrum two inches farther away from the head of the casket. Then he stepped carefully around the kneeler to move the candelabrum at the foot two inches. He had to step carefully, for there was very little room.

"A nice layout, sir," Snodgrass said.

Mr. Waddy knew it was a nice layout, the nicest he could devise. The casket was lined with the palest of shell pink, and they had found a dress of the same shade. It had been worth the trouble. Dannie looked like an angel asleep. And she would have complete privacy here. This little room, tucked in behind the stair well, was entirely removed from the usual range of visitors. Vince would be pleased.

"Snodgrass, will you make a call for me?" Mr. Waddy asked.
But Snodgrass had disappeared. Vaguely Mr. Waddy recol-
lected that the telephone had rung. When Snodgrass, a moment
later, called him to answer, he turned out the lights and closed
the door upon Dannie. He would give Vince a ring himself.

Mr. Waddy had rather been expecting Chief Wakeley to get
in touch with him and he was not surprised when the officer's
terse greeting came over the wire. What was a little surprising
was the question he rattled into Mr. Waddy's ear.

"Mr. Waddy, who is paying for Dannie Grear's funeral?"
The old gentleman closed his eyes and drew a long breath.
Wakeley was smart.

"Mr. Waddy?"

"Yes. Yes, Chief. I'm sorry."

"I asked you . . ."

"I know what you asked me. I cannot give you an answer."

"Why not?"

"Because, sir, I must not divulge private information. A
mortician must maintain the same code as a lawyer or a doctor.
The dead have no dignity except what the living preserve for
them. Perhaps the police hold to the same belief?"

There was a short pause.

"I'm going to have this information, Mr. Waddy. You'll have
to give it to me if I get a court order."

"I realize that, sir."

"Then I'll get it!"

Without the formality of a good-by, the line went dead.
Slowly Mr. Waddy replaced the receiver. Judge Deever
would have to issue the order and he was out at his summer
cabin. The order couldn't come through until tomorrow. No
need to be concerned about it. Take care of the other matter
first. He put his finger into a hole ready to dial a number
when the gong for the front door stroked the quiet.

"I'll get it, Snodgrass," Mr. Waddy called.

But before he could do so the door opened, admitted a man, and closed. Mr. Waddy was disturbed. The sign over the bell outside advised the visitor to ring and enter but this one hadn't waited even a second. And he was not a particularly soothing individual.

He was a big fellow. The sleeves of his black shirt were wrinkled, as if they had only recently been rolled down. The shirt was buttoned to the collar but he wore no tie. He had, in fact, the remains of mud on his blue jeans.

"Yes, sir?" Mr. Waddy inquired, putting a frown in his voice.

The fellow looked him up and down. "You're Henry Waddy?"

"I am."

"I'd like to see Dannie Grear."

Mr. Waddy returned the scrutiny in silence. His was not the only undertaking establishment in town. It was the oldest. And the best, naturally. But that was no reason why this unruly looking stranger should assume that Dannie should be here.

"I want to see if I can identify her," the man added.

"That will not be necessary, sir. The police are already satisfied as to her identity."

Mr. Waddy took a step forward, definitely suggesting that the unkempt boots should remove themselves from his good gray carpeting.

But the fellow didn't budge.

"The identification is for my own satisfaction, not for the police."

Mr. Waddy merely folded his arms. The fellow would have to do better than that.

The strong, darkly bearded chin lowered a trifle; the eyes, gray and cold, remained upon Mr. Waddy. If he had combed his hair he had done a poor job. But artistically poor. Something about him — the set of his head, that wild hair — something tugged at Mr. Waddy's memory.

The eyes narrowed. "I'm a tramp," the man said, and there was the viciousness in it of old tempers. "A carnival tramp. I make figures out of mud down on the water front."

"So that's where I've seen you," Mr. Waddy said. "Not this summer, though."

"This summer."

The old gentleman shook his head. "No. I haven't taken the time to visit the carnival this season."

"I've never been on the water front before this summer."

Mr. Waddy's plump shoulders lifted. It did seem much longer ago. Surely he couldn't have forgotten a recent visit to the river because Mrs. Waddy would have objected strongly and he never went anywhere like that without her.

"Pico, Pico della Mara," the fellow added. "But you wouldn't know my name. Nobody does. I'm 'hey, you,' down there."

"No," said Mr. Waddy, "no, that name is not familiar at all. But — about Miss Grear?"

"She stopped to admire my work. That is, I believe it was her. The cops were around this morning asking questions. I'd like to be sure."

"Didn't they describe her to you?"

"Listen!" the fellow began roughly, and immediately amended his tone. "Listen, do you have any idea the number of people stop during a day? Even if I model one of those dinky mud heads of them, I couldn't tell you what they looked like a minute later. All I know is they pay me a buck. Think the cop can understand that? No, he gets sore because I can't say right, right, right, she's the one. Burned me up! I'll drop by and see her, I told him, that's the only way I'll be sure. And he says O.K."

Mr. Waddy could reasonably hesitate no longer. He couldn't

quite restrain another glance at the dirty boots. But he led the way around the stairs to the small room, opened the door, and snapped on the light. The fellow, he hoped, would be content to glance in over his shoulder.

But he wasn't. Pushing past Mr. Waddy, he went over close to the casket. The candles were not lighted but even without their softness Dannie was a wax angel. The man took a long time to look at her.

"It's her," he said. "Dannie — what was her name?"

"Grear," Mr. Waddy said softly. "Dannie Grear."

His hand was on the light switch. He was not going to permit this carnival tramp to remain any longer than necessary within the clean confines of his establishment.

Chapter Nine

JINNY was alone. Posed on the end of Sybil's bed, she could see herself in the mirror. The orchid dress was thin as a cloud and embroidered in white, and her hair fell in shining blond waves to her shoulders. Sybil had given her a skillful make-up of lavender eye shadow, a touch of rouge for the china shepherdess effect, but no powder.

"Roger will eat you up," Sybil said as she departed on a date of her own. "He'll be back for more, I promise you. And don't try to talk much, just open your eyes wide. The mascara will do the rest."

Now that Sybil was gone, Jinny was so frightened her stomach felt like an empty bubble under the tight-fitting bodice; but she practiced opening her eyes wide. It all seemed a little silly. She'd give anything if she didn't have to go.

"Carter!" someone called out in the hall. "Hey, Liz, telephone!"

Jinny bounded off the bed and over to the door.

"Tony, don't call her! She's asleep!"

"I know it. I see her note on the board. But this guy really wants her."

"Is it Ted?"

"No, some other fellow." Antonia, wrapped in a large towel,

85

grabbed a corner as it slipped. "You talk to him, will you, Jin? I'm dripping all over. Wow, do you look scrumptious!"

"I feel awful," Jinny said. "I wish you'd hurry up and get some clothes on. The monitor isn't supposed to run around like that. And you're supposed to put Roger in the mush room when he comes."

"Sybil told me. I'll be there in a fresh paint job."

"Then hurry up!"

"O.K., O.K. But you answer that creature before he blows a fuse."

Tony pattered away. Jinny took up the telephone.

"Hello," she said. "This is . . ."

"Lizette? Listen carefully. I'll only explain this once."

The voice was not Ted's. It was low and gruff, fearfully commanding.

"Lizette, can you hear me?"

"Yes," she quavered. "Yes, but . . ."

"All right. Now get this straight. Go to the laundromat, the Snow White. Do you know where that is?"

"Yes." The time was past for telling him she was not Lizette.

"The woman, Dannie Grear, left her suitcase there. I want it. You go to the Snow White and get it, then bring it down to the water front. Be sure you come down the stairs with a crowd, not alone. You don't want to be noticed. Put the suitcase back under the stairs. Then leave. Got it straight?"

"I think so."

"Don't tell anybody where you're going and don't bring anybody with you." There was a second's pause. "If you double-cross me on this, you'll wish you hadn't. And you'll never live to identify me, remember that. The only way we'll get along is for you to play ball. Understand?"

"Yes."

The little word was only a whisper, but he must have heard

it for the line went dead. Jinny let the receiver fall in place. She was oddly numb. Not frightened, just numb. Slowly she walked back to Sybil's room, her high heels tapping. In the room she closed the door, sat down on the end of the bed, and folded her hands. A beautiful girl in an orchid dress looked back at her from the mirror.

The girl had just talked to Dannie Grear's murderer.

She stared into the mirror while cold paralysis held her body and brain. One small thought broke through: Gordie was right. The murderer did believe that Lizette could identify him. So that put Lizette in the same peril Dannie Grear had faced. And Dannie was dead.

The clock ticked busily through empty minutes. Time might be precious, for the man sounded as if he expected his order to be carried out instantly. Not that Jinny needed time to decide what to do. From almost the first minute, she knew. Liz was her best friend, her defender and her rescuer times without number. Liz would be in very real danger if she were to take the suitcase down under the stairs, because the man might go back on his promise to play ball. After all, he had killed once, and to kill again would not make him any worse off than he was already.

"I can't! I simply can't!" Jinny whispered.

But this was a chance to do something for Lizette. The one-sided friendship would be well balanced, even tipped to Jinny's side, for nothing in the world was so important as saving a life. And that was what she would be doing for Liz. She herself would be in no danger. She didn't know the man.

She jumped up and started to unzip the dress. But why take it off? She wouldn't be gone forever and upon her return she would be ready to go out with Roger. He would have to wait a little but he was used to waiting for Sybil. And she could ask Tony to explain. . . .

She couldn't. Don't tell anyone where you're going, the man had said. Glancing out of the window, she saw that the sidewalk was empty of everything except a few dragonflies darning a pattern over the petunias. A quarter to seven. Roger would come around seven. Being conditioned to Sybil, he would wait until half past without getting the fidgets, and by that time Jinny would be back. She snatched the pretty beaded purse Sybil had lent her. In it were fifty cents on lend-lease from Evvie, a lipstick, comb, handkerchief, and her rosary, all the temporal and spiritual insurance she would need for the evening.

Tiptoeing out into the hall as if she must sneak past a dozen spies, Jinny headed for the alley entrance. Voices came from rooms, but there was no one to see her go. Perhaps no one would see her come back, either, and the secret of this great thing she was doing for Lizette would be her own until she would choose to tell it.

Right at the doorway, she met Sister Simon coming in.

Sister Simon took a second glance before she recognized the girl in the orchid dress.

"Jinny, how lovely you look! That color is heavenly on you."

She paused then. Was she not saying the right thing? In the girl's eyes there was an expression of fear. She glanced at her watch. The time could have nothing to do with it. All the girls off duty were free in the evening.

"Thank you, Sister," Jinny was murmuring. "I . . . it isn't mine . . . I'm going . . . good-by, 'Ster!"

"Have a good time, dear. Is Lizette in her room?"

"Yes, 'Ster. But she's asleep."

The nun, on the steps, watched the blond hair flying as Jinny ran away down the alley toward the street. Some little mission she didn't want discovered, no doubt something so harmless you'd wonder why she had bothered to cover it up. Smiling to herself, Sister Simon walked down the alley past the emergency entrance and on across to the convent. She would have preferred to have her talk with Lizette, but since it had to be postponed she was relieved. Tomorrow, perhaps, would be even better. She might not be so tired. There was still work that could be done, of course, paperwork up on pedes. But where did duty end and martyrdom begin? She couldn't remember exactly when she had gone to recreation. Tonight, in the close family company of the nuns, she would forget the cares that nagged her, and finally she would be able to sleep.

She was thinking about her crocheting as she climbed the steps to the lumberman's porch. In the chest in the recreation room, it seemed she had left it there. She couldn't remember exactly what she was making, either a doily or a chair cover, pineapple design, for her niece Betty. It didn't really matter. Betty was not likely to use it anyway in her modernistic living room. . . .

"Simon?"

Old Sister Joe was getting up out of a rocker, leaving it to whack against another, coming forward with a step that shook the porch. She must have been waiting for me, Sister Simon thought, she wants to know more about the murder. The old nun took her by the arm.

"Sister, will you come with me to the mortuary? I must see her."

"See who, Sister?"

"Dannie Grear."

"I can tell you about her. We wouldn't have to . . ."

The wrinkled face came closer, and the voice took on anxiety.

"I have permission, Sister. Mother is so very kind. She says we may use the car. It's not only that you can drive, Sister, but this morning you told me — I'm sure you told me about Dannie. I couldn't forget that, could I, dear?"

"Oh, no, no, I told you," Sister Simon replied quickly. She wanted nothing less than to go to Henry Waddy's and look at a dead woman, but she added, making the gesture that would explain her words, "I'll have to change into my black habit, Sister."

The old nun nodded. "I didn't do anything for her when she asked me to, dear. You see, I thought, when we could talk — well, we never can, now. But I'd like to pay my respects to her. You understand, Sister?"

"Oh, of course," Sister Simon answered, unpinning a sleeve.

"She was Damian when she was with us," Sister Joe remarked. The pin bit into the young nun's thumb. "I knew she wouldn't stay. Even without the fire, she wouldn't have stayed. Now run along, dear. Mother won't like it if we're out too late."

With her thumb in her mouth, Sister Simon hurried into the cloister.

The Snow White was a bedlam of thunderously churning machines when Jinny entered and sidled up to the counter. In the steamy rear a dozen women shouted companionably at one another as they stepped around piles of laundry. The girl attendant looked as if she had just been lifted out of a hot tub, clothes and all. She pushed a pad and pencil toward Jinny.

"Write it."

"What?"

"Name. I can't hear nothin' above them machines. Saves a lot of time if you write your name."

Jinny's heart gave a fearful leap. The man hadn't mentioned a name. If she were to say Dannie Grear, and the girl had read the papers — and who hadn't! — she would most likely call the police.

The girl swiped her face with the back of her wrist and leaned over the counter. "That's sure a pretty dress. But it won't wash. I don't buy nothin' won't wash. Only I'd sure like somethin' like that."

"Thank you," Jinny said. "I'm after a suitcase."

"A what?"

"Suitcase. I'm calling for it. The woman can't come."

The girl swiped her face with the other wrist. "They don't generally put their stuff in suitcases. Must be somethin' the boss took in."

"Please look!" Jinny begged. "I promised I'd get it!"

The girl drooped down under the counter, reappearing almost immediately with a small tweed paper suitcase.

"This it? Only one we got."

"Oh, that's it!" Jinny exclaimed. This was the one Liz had described, tweedy and poor. "Thank you so much!"

"Wait a minute. Let's see how much I collect."

"Collect?"

"We ain't in business for fun, ma'am."

Jinny knew a moment of panic, then. She had fifty cents. What if the charge should be more? Was the whole success of this mission — Lizette's very life — to hang on a few cents she didn't have?

The girl found a slip of paper stuck to the side of the suitcase, read it, and shrugged.

"No charge. He must of felt softhearted, for some reason. Well, there you go."

She pushed the suitcase across the counter. Jinny grabbed the small handle.

"I just don't know how to thank you!"

"Don't bother. I ain't used to it." The girl smiled. "You been in here before with another student nurse. Real cute."

"That's Lizette. Good-by, and thanks again."

"Goin' out on a date, huh? Have fun."

"Oh, I will!"

Out on the sidewalk Jinny wondered briefly how the girl knew they were nurses, started to run, then slowed to a walk. People would look at her, dashing by. She must be inconspicuous, stay with this crowd, and perhaps when they reached the boat company's big building enough of them would go down the stairs to make a cover for her. She had obeyed orders to the letter, thus far. And it hadn't been so difficult. She felt strong and courageous when, at the top of the stairs, she looked down on the river park.

Mr. Waddy knew he should go home. Twice since six o'clock Mrs. Waddy had called, urging him to end his long day. He would have done so gladly if it weren't for his conviction that he would only carry his restlessness home with him, and he couldn't face a new frontier of sympathy. The boys had borne with his anxieties all day, kindly and for the most part wordlessly. But they had shown their concern. Ted, for instance, had rushed back on his supper break, stood on one leg for a moment before Mr. Waddy, and then dashed to the kitchenette to start the percolator. Snodgrass had been brewing coffee all afternoon and Mr. Waddy had meekly drunk so much that by the time Ted came in with his tray he had worked up quite a case of sour stomach. But he couldn't turn the boy down.

Susan, whose mind was normally on something entirely extra-curricular, even forgot to repair her lipstick. Mr. Waddy hadn't been so fortunate in keeping secretaries — they were all either too thrilled or too awed by the surroundings — but Susan Chapin had been here quite a while now. She was a good girl. Each time Mr. Waddy entered the office today her fingers would trip over the statements she was typing, and her large eyes would fasten on him, brimming with concern. At five o'clock, however, Susan departed. Snodgrass disappeared, and the place became so quiet that the old gentleman, who had been longing for solitude, found he could not bear his own company.

It was around seven fifteen when he wandered through the hall past the preparation room and the kitchenette and out into the garage. Young Lombard was there, shining up the hearse although his hours of duty were over long ago. He waved to Mr. Waddy with an alert air of fellow feeling. They wanted to help, all of them. The old gentleman's vision clouded a little. He'd certainly explain as soon as possible.

"Very nice, Gene," he said. "Don't forget the steering wheel. We must have it all perfect for tomorrow."

For tomorrow. For Dannie. He had been saying things like that all day. Really, he must be quite a trial to have around.

Very quietly, so as not to arouse Snodgrass with another cup of coffee, Mr. Waddy re-entered the passageway, went safely past the kitchenette, and reached the front lobby. Two nuns, one extremely tall and broad and old, the other young and pretty, stood just inside the front door. They were all in black, even their hands, and their white coifs made shadows around their faces.

"Yes. Good evening, Sisters," Mr. Waddy said. He had the queer feeling that this had happened before, long ago. . . .

"I am Sister Mary Joseph," the tall one said very loudly. Deaf, of course. "This is Sister Mary Simon. We have come to pay our respects to Damian."

"Dannie Grear," the younger nun added.

It was fitting that nuns should come to pray for Dannie, so fitting that Mr. Waddy didn't waste a wonder on the new name. Not exactly new, either. Like the appearance of the tall Sister, it rang a faint bell.

He opened the door of the small room, snapped on a shaded lamp, and stood aside. They went straight to the casket and knelt. Mr. Waddy folded his hands. Dannie looked so young. Perhaps all the soft pink helped the illusion. But it was the way he had laid her out, too, giving that tiny tilt to the head that no one had ever discovered and yet it made all the difference between funereal stiffness and the impression of natural sleep.

The tall nun, Sister Joseph, rose from her knees. She had been crying. Mr. Waddy liked her for it.

"Poor Damian. I'd know her anywhere," she said. "She had a beautiful life, you can tell that. She made no mistake, leaving us."

The memory snapped to the surface of Mr. Waddy's muddled mind. "Of course! You were the Mother Superior then! I remember!" He held out his hand.

Sister Joe smiled, a miracle of wrinkled pleasure, and took his hand in both of hers. "You've done a beautiful job, Mr. Waddy. Why, she looks as young as the day she entered the convent!"

Mr. Waddy smiled tremulously.

"She seemed to be so uncertain while she was with us," the old nun went on, and her eyes returned to Dannie. The younger one still knelt. "She didn't belong in the convent. I knew it, but she had to find out for herself. Girls come in for all kinds of reasons besides the right one, and they always find out. She had been disappointed in love."

"I know," Mr. Waddy said.

"You remember Elizabeth? I never thought she was quite fair with Damian. She didn't like Steve, you know, she thought he was a ne'er-do-well — and of course he was. So she told Damian that Steve was about to marry someone else. You never heard whether he actually did, I suppose?"

Sister Joseph was looking at him, and Mr. Waddy shook his head. His hands, clasped behind him, were wet with perspiration.

"Well, it might not have worked out, anyway. So much tragedy, all related somehow to Steve. You have to wonder, sometimes, why the Lord permits these things to happen."

"Not Steve," Mr. Waddy said. "Steve wasn't good."

Sister Joseph went right on, not having heard him. "I've often thought how providential it was that Elizabeth brought the baby to the convent that day. If she hadn't, the child would surely have been burned up with her. You know Diane? A beautiful girl. I gave Damian permission to keep her for the day. As it happened, she kept her for twenty-one years."

"A wonderful sacrifice," the old gentleman murmured. The Sister must have read his lips, for she replied.

"Not a sacrifice in the ordinary sense, Mr. Waddy. There was nothing Damian wanted when she couldn't have Steve. That was why she entered the convent, and it was why she left. The baby took Steve's place in her heart." Sister Joe paused. "I've been looking over my old scrapbook, you see, and it's all back with me so clearly. The hunting accident, that was the beginning. Perhaps nothing would have happened if they hadn't gone hunting that time."

"Perhaps not," Mr. Waddy whispered.

Sister Simon crossed herself and rose from her knees.

"Yes, we must go," Sister Joseph said in her customary boom. "Thank you for your kindness, sir."

"Not at all." Mr. Waddy, bowing, stood aside. "Could one of the boys give you a ride home?"

The old nun's eyes twinkled. "In the hearse, sir? Thank you, no, I'll be in it soon enough. We have our own car."

Mr. Waddy murmured politely and went through his usual handshaking. But when he had closed the outer door behind the nuns, he sat down on the first chair he could reach. Once, on a country hike, he had been caught in a hailstorm and the effect of being pelted with ice was like this. He had crawled into a thicket, and the tangle of branches had somewhat broken the battering downfall. There was no thicket here.

Voices sounded from the direction of the kitchenette, something about coffee. Mr. Waddy got to his feet and went as quickly as he could manage up the stairs to his office. It was cool and dusky there, tranquil as a woodsy dell. Buzzing the house phone he told Snodgrass, in the kitchen, that he and young Lombard might leave now. No, indeed, there was nothing more for them to do. He himself would be here until Ted Benedict returned at eleven. Then he sat down at his desk, snapped on a light, and opened his Bible.

"How long, ye simple ones, will ye love simplicity, and the scorners delight in their scorning, and fools hate knowledge?" Wise old Solomon! Wearily Mr. Waddy rubbed his hand over his eyes. How long? Only until tomorrow morning, ten o'clock, even nine. Judge Deever was an early riser, and Wakeley wouldn't dally about getting the court order.

Pulling the telephone toward him, Mr. Waddy fingered the dial. He dialed one number, then broke the connection. Outside on the avenue Lombard's jallopy started up with a loud series of reports. Loyalty was a touching thing. Although sometimes misplaced. Again Mr. Waddy picked up the phone and began to dial. Vince Barron, having about as rancid a nature as any human being ever possessed, might not understand or appreciate loyalty; but he had always leaned on it, taken it as his right from his friend Henry.

The Bible had flipped shut. Mr. Waddy's eyes rested on the worn black cover. In his ear the bell ringing in a far-off room made an insistent summons.

Like a diver out of ocean depths, Lizette struggled out of sleep. The ceiling light was on full in her eyes and someone was shaking her awake.

"Cut it out," she mumbled, "Le' me alone." And she tried to roll over to bury her face in the pillow.

But the shaking went on.

"Liz, wake up! You've got to tell me where she is!"

"Where who is?"

"Jinny."

"She's out on a date. Turn off that darn light!"

"Liz, she *didn't go* out with Roger! Come on, wake up!"

Determined palms slapped her cheeks. Fighting them off, Lizette came awake. Tony was crouched on the side of the bed, her round face anxious.

"We can't find her anywhere, Liz. She's skun out."

"Maybe she didn't like the looks of Roger."

"She didn't even take a peek at him. I felt sorry for the poor guy, stood up by two girls in one night. He sat in the mush room nearly an hour, waiting."

"And Jinny didn't show up?"

"No. And she looked absolutely ambrosial. She was all ready when she came out to . . . "

Tony broke off as if someone had knocked her breathless.

"Came out to what, Tony?"

"To answer the phone. Oh, Liz, that couldn't have anything to do with her disappearance, could it?"

Chill fingers ran down Lizette's spine. "Maybe you'd better tell me the beginning, the middle, and the end. What phone call?"

"It was for you. I answered first."

"Who was it?"

"I don't know. A man. Come to think about it, I didn't like the sound of him one bit!"

"Now don't imagine things, Tony," Lizette said sternly. "Why didn't you call me?"

"Because you'd left a note on the board, no calls. I let out one yell and Jinny came running and said she'd take it. And — that's all."

That was all. A call from a strange man who didn't sound nice. And this afternoon there had been Evvie's talk about her brother-in-law's opinions, and a heated discussion about friendship — I'd do anything for Liz, Jinny had said — and tonight she was gone.

"You're thinking something, Liz," Tony accused. "You're scared!"

"What is there to be scared of?" Lizette asked, but she jumped out of bed and began to gather clothes. "What time is it?"

"Almost ten thirty."

"She goes on duty at eleven. I bet she's in Sybil's room right now, getting dressed. She doesn't want to disturb me."

"She isn't there."

"Maybe she left a note for me out on the board."

"No. I looked."

"Try over on the desk."

Tony bounced across the room. "I don't see anything. Boy, what a mess!"

She paused, frowning. "Liz, I just thought of something! If she took off the orchid dress, wouldn't that mean . . . well, she didn't intend to come back?"

Lizette, rummaging in a drawer for a clean slip, sat back on her heels. "Possibly. But where would she go?"

Tony gave a large shrug. "Sybil isn't in yet, either. I'll scan her closet."

"Grab me a cap from somebody, too, will you? Mine has spinach on it."

Tony bounded away. Lizette began to put the buttons in a fresh uniform. But her fingers trembled so badly she made slow headway, and a peculiar emptiness began to stir at the pit of her stomach. Would it bode ill or good if the orchid dress was in the closet?

"Not there," Tony reported, coming in to toss a cap on the bed. "That's one of mine."

"Then she'll be back. She'd never risk a demerit for being late, much less a whole flock of them for absence."

"Not with the queen business coming up," Tony agreed. "Why didn't we think of that before?"

The assurance, however, had worn thin by the time Lizette reached the nurses' station on pediatrics. There had been no telephone call from Jinny frantically begging that Liz cover up for her until she could arrive, no note found hidden under a pillow or under the dresser scarf or pinned to the stuffed rooster. Lizette tried to work up a defensive impatience over Jinny's nonappearance. Anything was better than the fear that swelled and grew with every minute.

Poppy, going over the charts with the relief nurse, merely glanced up as Lizette came in.

"You're on the small end tonight, Carter. I'll let Johnson take the big kids."

Lizette nodded and said something. She and the aide could do all right since most of the young patients were asleep. Jinny could appear with an armful of diapers and the only reprimand would be for not reporting to the station when she came on duty. With any luck, it wouldn't occur to Poppy to inquire when she actually had come.

But a half hour went by and Lizette finally met Poppy head on in the utility room. Poppy came straight to the point.

"Where's Johnson?"

"Jinny?"

"Virginia. Your dear friend and roommate. I'm sure I'd of noticed if she was here. Something would of gone wrong. Is she sick?"

"No. Anyway, I don't think so."

"Just having herself a night off? Looky, this idea of putting in extra hours was hers, not mine, and I'm depending on her. I told the aide with the drinkin' husband not to come tonight."

"I'm sorry, Poppy. But Jinny'll get here."

"Well, if I have to dig her up she's gonna get a demerit."

Poppy filled a hot-water bottle and tipped it expertly to expel the air. Lizette, watching the water rise in the neck, made a sudden decision.

"She's gone, Poppy."

"Come again?"

"She got all dressed up for a date and then she disappeared."

"Got scared of the guy? Well, if that's it we won't be too hard on her. I sure remember my first glimpse of the character I married." Poppy slapped the bottle. "But with Jinny that Gooseberry Festival's so all-fired important. . . . "

"Blueberry."

"I could keep her from even seeing a blueberry, for this performance."

"It would break her heart, Poppy!"

"I know it. Well, let's make us a quick novena of nine minutes, see if St. Anthony can put a bug in her ear. I can't give her much longer."

"Midnight?"

"O.K., midnight."

"Poppy, you're a friend in need!"

"It's my Irish grandmother."

But midnight came and passed, and no one but an orderly came through the swinging door to pediatrics. Poppy, meeting Lizette at the station desk, glanced up at the clock.

"Time's run out, Liz. Five after."

"What will we do?"

"Call the nurses' home. I don't think she's there, but try. It'll be less official, coming from you."

Lizette made the call. Neither of them was surprised when a sleepy girl said no, Jinny hadn't come back. Poppy picked up a pencil and tapped on the desk absently.

"I could wring her neck sometimes," she said slowly, "but you've gotta admit she's the soul of faithfulness. Something big, fat, and important has sure come up, bigger'n the gooseberries. The question is — what?"

"Poppy, she took a telephone call for me. From a man."

"Swiped a date on you, you mean?"

"Not like that. Tony said he didn't sound a bit nice. But Jinny talked to him, and that's the last anybody saw of her."

Poppy leaned forward, her knees spread, and a button skipped off her uniform and across the floor.

"Liz, we might as well face it. Last night a woman was killed here, tonight a girl's missing. Maybe they have nothing to do with each other, but . . . " She spread her hands eloquently. "If Jinny's — well, in trouble, then the demerit won't count. And if she isn't, she deserves one. I'll give Simon a jingle."

Lizette stretched after the button and her face was hidden from Poppy. "Does it have to be — I mean, why not the police?"

"Oh, ducky, Sister would never forgive the slight to her authority if I called the cops on my own!"

"You'll wake the whole convent."

"So what?"

Poppy reached for the phone. Down the hall a child cried. Lizette jumped up. "There's that little Phelps demon. I better get him quick. Poppy, make it as light as you can, won't you?"

But Lizette knew, just as Poppy did, that the facts couldn't be lightened. For how could you minimize the fact that a girl who was the soul of faithfulness, who wouldn't risk her cherished reign as Blueberry Queen for anything in the world — that girl had thrown faithfulness and caution to the winds and was unaccountably missing?

Chapter Ten

SISTER SIMON sat with the old scrapbook open on her lap. She was not looking at it. Her hand lay on the pasted clippings, her eyes were unseeing upon the pillow where her tired head should have been resting for the past two hours. Her shoes stood side by side at the foot of the bed, but she still wore her black habit. Her mind was filled with what she had just read. "It's all here, dear," Sister Joe had said. And no doubt it was, if you knew what to make of it. Two tragedies, both accidental, had touched Dannie Grear, changing the course of her life completely; and twenty years later Dannie herself was murdered. In every life the present is somehow the harvest of the past. How often her policeman father used to say that! Was it possible that here, on these brown old pages, the planting of the deadly seed was recorded?

I don't really want to know, Sister Simon thought; yet her eyes again sought the headline, "Hunter Accidentally Shot Near Beechwood Falls, Brother Missing," and underneath it the smaller line, "James McArthur, Fourth Fatality of Season." Somebody named Willis Lawrence had also disappeared on the same night Jim McArthur was shot. The reporter ended with a remark about the awful toll of lives during the deer hunting season. So impersonal in print, so hurtfully personal to Elizabeth and Diane. And Dannie?

Out in the hall the telephone rang. The nun was instantly on her feet. In the daytime the ring would be a routine interruption, but at night it was the sharp rap of emergency. Sister Simon made such good time that she cut off the third ring. It was Poppy. Virginia hadn't come on duty. No one had seen her since sometime around six thirty.

"Then she didn't come back?" the nun asked needlessly.

"Back from where, Sister?"

"I met her at the door at a quarter to seven. She didn't say where she was going."

"Well, all we know is she took a telephone call intended for Lizette, and then she disappeared. I think you better call the police, Sister. She's sure not staying off of her own accord, not with that blueberry business coming up."

"I'll call Wakeley."

It was all Sister Simon could say because the pounding of her heart was suffocating. She stood for a long minute staring at the newel post, trying to get her breath. So she hadn't been mistaken about the fear in Jinny's eyes. The girl had been on her way to do something that frightened her to death. . . . To death? Would there be another headline tomorrow or the next day, "Body of Missing Girl Found. . . ?"

Her trembling hands dropped the phone book, and she at last fumbled out Wakeley's number. He answered in a voice thick with sleep.

"If she's out on a date, wouldn't that explain it? Kids lose track of time."

"Not Virginia. And she was afraid! I saw her go!"

There was a short pause. When Wakeley's voice came again it had snapped to attention.

"All right, Sister. I'll get out a bulletin and then I'll be over to the hospital. Give me a rundown on what she looks like, what she was wearing, anything that would help us spot her."

The description, the nun knew, was the merest outside of Jinny. What had happened on the inside to make her disappear? Was it something concerning the call she had taken for Lizette? Was she still running, her lovely orchid dress billowing out? Fleeing away from something . . . or toward some person or thing only she knew about? All the policemen and highway patrolmen and sheriff's deputies within two hundred miles, Wakeley was saying, would be alerted, they'd find her, don't worry.

"Thank you," the Sister said, and hurried back to her cell to put on her shoes. She was out in the hall again when she stopped, turned back, and took the old scrapbook from the bed where she had dropped it. Then, with it under her arm, she went noiselessly out of the convent and over to the hospital. Come to the visitors' waiting room on the first floor, she had told Wakeley. The room was dark and empty. Going on to the switchboard, she instructed Evvie to call pediatrics and ask Poppy to come down.

"O.K., Sister," Evvie said, but she didn't reach for the plug. Her brown eyes were wide and frightened, and her midnight sandwich lay in the wax paper with one bite out of it. "Sister, couldn't we maybe lock that front door at night? It's awful public, I mean, anybody can come in. I mean . . . "

"There's nothing to be afraid of, Evvie," the Sister said sternly. "Dannie Grear's death had no connection with us."

"Well . . . but where's Jinny?"

"She'll be back. Now don't worry."

"The cop's comin' though, ain't he?"

Sister Simon pressed her lips together, decided not to call Evvie down for listening in on her telephone conversation, and answered briefly, "Yes, he's coming."

"That darn ivy is what bothers me, that's what it is!" Evvie went on. "We were talking about it this afternoon and I was telling the kids how it swung . . . Sister! There it goes again!"

The delicate tendrils were swaying above the arch but there was no sound of anyone entering, an eerie performance indeed if one were alone, and watching.

"Don't be so silly, Evvie! It's Chief Wakeley, naturally."

The Sister said it firmly enough. But she was not totally without doubt herself until she came right to the door of the waiting room and saw the Chief switching on a light. The good solid size of him was most heartening. Even in the self-containment of the convent, she thought as she seated herself on the brink of a settee, there was a certain dependence on the strength of a man.

Wakeley was alert and fresh, his black hair smoothly shining and every button properly buttoned.

"Now about this girl," he began, and stopped when Lizette appeared in the archway. "Oh, Miss Carter."

"Poppy sent me, Sister," said Lizette. "I know more about this than she does."

"Of course, dear. Sit here."

She patted the settee; but Lizette dropped into the nearest chair. The Sister clasped her hands on the scrapbook in her lap. If the tight, quick way in which the girl began answering Wakeley's questions was any indication, she was very near the breaking point. How sinful was my neglect, Sister Simon thought as she listened. I should have had a talk with her today. This tension is my fault. Yet, with the development of the story, another reason for the tension became evident: the girls, Evvie in particular, had been very certain that Lizette herself was in danger.

"Because the man — whoever killed Dannie Grear — might think I saw him on the water front and I could identify him.

But I can't! I didn't see anyone suspicious!" Lizette's voice shook to a whisper. Her hands were so tightly clenched that the knuckles were white. "And Jinny said she would do anything for me, and then this call came and I know it's what sent her out, wherever she's gone. And he's done something to her, that's why she hasn't come back! She *can't!*"

Wakeley took out his pencil. "Did anyone else know about the call?"

"The girl who answered the phone. Tony Burke. She'd just got out of the shower so she called Jinny. I was asleep."

He wrote the name on a folded paper.

"You can't just write things!" Lizette cried. "Don't you understand, he'll kill her if you don't find her right away!"

"We're looking for her already, Miss Carter. But it might help if we knew why she went off."

"I've told you why! She's protecting me!"

"Possibly so. Well, we'll know when we find her."

Wakeley shoved the folded paper into his pocket and made a movement to rise.

"Officer," Sister Simon said, for it was now or never. "Officer, have you looked into Dannie's past at all?"

"Of course, Sister."

"And what did you learn?"

"She had a very routine life, clerked in a store in Beechwood Falls for eighteen years, some friends, nothing out of the ordinary."

"But farther back than that?"

"She grew up here in the Narrows, went to school, the usual thing."

"Do you know about the accident — two accidents, really, that placed Diane in her care?"

"The girl herself mentioned them."

"It's more important than a mention." Sister Simon tapped the picture of Niagara Falls on the cover of the scrapbook. "Sister Joseph — she was Mother then — kept clippings from the local papers. There's something here, I'm sure of it!"

"You may be right, Sister. There's always a high road and a low road to the solution of every case. I could dig into the past and probably in the course of time come up with something, but it would be a long process. In the first place I'd have to hunt up everybody connected with Dannie Grear — how long ago was it, twenty years? And they're scattered to the winds, maybe even dead. That's the long road. The short cut is to find out who followed Dannie up here from the water front. Somebody saw him, somewhere. The suitcase and purse are somewhere, too. So . . . " Wakeley spread his hands, palms up, "find the suitcase or the purse, or a witness who can give us a clue or two, and there we are."

"Or find out where Jinny went," Lizette added. "That would be the shortest cut of all!"

"It's a possibility, Miss Carter, nothing more." The Chief made another movement to rise.

"Please!"

Sister Simon was faintly surprised at the urgency of her own exclamation, a surprise she saw reflected in Wakeley's pause.

"Yes, Sister?"

She felt her cheeks growing warm. Why should she hesitate to put her theory before him? Hadn't she heard tales of the detection of crime from her father in place of bedtime stories ever since she could remember? He might knock her idea into a cocked hat, but . . .

"Will you listen just a minute, please?" she begged. "It's all in my head, so I can tell you quickly. Jim McArthur was Diane's father, the one who was killed in the hunting accident. And the same night, Jim's younger brother, Steve vanished. Steve had been with the hunting party."

"If you have all the clippings, Sister, you know what happened to him. Seven or eight years later, some geologist out on a scouting expedition found his skeleton in a ravine. So if there was any suspicion attached to Steve, that's where it ended."

"But the other tragedy — Diane's mother Elizabeth burned to death. And only three weeks later!"

"In a fire that swept in from the woods. Half the countryside was aflame that fall, one of the worst years in history for forest fires. No, Sister." Wakeley got to his feet this time. "No, it was just one of those things. The only connection with Dannie Grear was that the double tragedy landed the baby in her lap."

"Dannie was in the convent at the time. She left to care for Diane."

"Too bad."

He said it casually. The emotional conflict involved in such a decision was beyond his ken. If he had a thought at all it would probably be that with Dannie's departure Mother would have been short of help to scrub the floors. A rush of explanation flooded to Sister Simon's tongue — but what good would it do to try to explain to a nonbeliever at one o'clock in the morning?

The Chief said good night and took himself off. Over in the corner Lizette got up, ready to fly away.

"Lizette."

"Yes, 'Ster."

The nun rose and walked across the room to face the girl. Lizette remained looking down the hall as if something of great importance had caught her attention, but there was no heart, really, to her stiffness. She's ashamed, the Sister thought, ashamed and obstinate and terribly hurt. Her eyes were red from crying. Jinny was her friend.

"Lizette, I was reading St. Augustine tonight. About duty. He says, 'In doing what we ought we deserve no praise, because it is our duty.' And the reverse is also true. In doing what we ought we deserve no blame. Think about it, dear."

Lizette pressed her lips tight together. But she was not being stubborn now, she was trying hard not to break down. The nun went on evenly, addressing the urn out of which the ivy grew.

"I believe the Chief is wrong. It seems to me the real short cut is through this." She tapped the scrapbook which she held in her folded arms. "If we could find out *why*, then surely we would know *who*. There must be a link somewhere."

As she spoke, something teased her memory, perhaps a name she had skipped over in her reading. Frowning in concentration, she sat down and opened the book. She scanned the first of the clippings which was the bare report of the shooting accident. Nothing there. But at the end of the second article the names of the other hunters were given. Her finger stopped under the last.

"For goodness' sake!"

"What is it, Sister?"

"Henry Waddy! He was one of the hunters!"

"Henry Waddy?" The girl dropped down beside the nun. "Sister, he must have been a good friend of Dannie's! Ted told me the poor old guy was absolutely knocked out when he saw her on the stretcher. Do you think . . . Sister, what *do* you think?"

I'm thinking how blessed it is that the barrier between us has fallen, the nun might have said. But she shook her head.

"I'm not thinking anything yet, Lizette. But couldn't it be that he's our link?"

"Oh, but he wouldn't kill her!"

"He might know who did."

"He couldn't be mixed up in murder! He's so gentle and so cute. . . ."

"And so worried. We were at the mortuary tonight, Sister Joseph and I. And Mr. Waddy was . . . not frightened. . . . Heartsick, that's the right word. Sick right to the heart."

"And you think it was about Dannie?"

"I have no way of knowing. I'd soon find out if I could talk to him. Only how could I?"

"I can talk to him, Sister."

"Of course you can."

Sister Simon responded almost automatically. But you don't send young girls chasing after possible clues to murder. You call up the policeman — the policeman who already has said he will not delve into the past?

"We're talking foolishness, dear," the nun said, closing the book. "This is definitely no business of ours."

"We've made it our business because we both feel guilty about not helping Dannie."

Before the Sister could gather her nice assortment of facts concerning duty, Lizette hurried on.

"Whether we admit it or not, it's true, and the only way we'll get to feel better is to *do* something. And it would be so easy, Sister!" The girl laid her hand on the Sister's arm. "My boy friend, Ted Benedict, is Waddy's night man, and I can stop by and ask for him. He'll find a casual way to talk to Mr. Waddy. There'd be nothing to it, Sister!"

"Well . . . but when can you go?"

"As soon as I'm off duty. Ted said he'd be over at seven. He'll go back with me."

"Make it a little earlier, then, and catch him before he leaves. I'll come and help Poppy for that last half hour."

"Oh, thank you, Sister! Now tell me what to ask Mr. Waddy."

"All about the accidents, both of them. Who went on the hunting trip, exactly how Jim McArthur was shot, everything he knows about the fire. And about Steve."

"I don't see where Steve comes in," Lizette said. "Anyway, not after they found his bones."

Not after they found his bones. The little phrase hung in her mind as Sister Simon went back to the convent. Steve was dead. The geologist couldn't have run across his bones unless he was dead. Steve belonged to the past. In the present there was a more immediate concern: knowing that Mother Richard would never allow even the slightest participation in a murder investigation, was she begging the question of obedience by sending Lizette to talk with Henry Waddy? St. Augustine, it seemed, had the answer. She had read it this evening. "Let the superior be obeyed like a mother, with all due honor, so that you offend not God through offending her." But how could Mother be offended through a short friendly conversation she would never hear about? For that was all it would amount to. Kind, benign Mr. Waddy would assure Lizette that the stories were exactly as stated in the clippings, two regrettable accidents, and Chief Wakeley would go straight along his high road to the solution of the mystery. Lizette herself would know the satisfaction of having done something for Dannie Grear. And Sister Simon would share the satisfaction.

Sighing deeply, she closed the cloister door behind her. In four hours the rising bell would ring. The only thought she would carry to bed with her was the reassuring one that the chip had fallen from Lizette's shoulder.

Chapter Eleven

THE morning, at twenty minutes to seven, was ideal summer. Hurrying across the river bridge, Lizette was only half conscious of the clean air and the quiet. She was thinking as she had been doing all night of Sister Simon and of Jinny. The police had not called, and their silence spoke loudly that no trace had been found of the missing girl. Her thoughts concerning Sister Simon were not so well defined. She should have understood the nun's adherence to duty, for very often she was overscrupulous herself. But when the rules hurt *you*, that's when they should be relaxed. Not for anyone else, only for you. And because the Sister hadn't made an exception for her, Lizette was bitterly resentful. That was most unfair. Still, when you remembered that the exception might have saved Dannie's life . . .

Lizette looked up abruptly from the pavement, for she was not going around that narrow, exasperating little race track again. Main Street was unnatural without its crowd of vacationers. The mind reader's tent on the portico of the Nickelodeon Palace was fastened shut. Down at the docks the excursion boats lay with their awnings furled and chairs tipped upside down on the decks. A solitary dog barked among the trailers, a few trucks roared by, pigeons walked cooing and nodding after yesterday's popcorn in the gutters. In the shooting gallery, wide open to the street, a colored boy was doing a lackadaisical job of sweeping. Farther along a girl with her head tied up in a bandana was giving a swish or two to the windows of the launderette.

"Oh, hi," the girl said as Lizette approached.

"Hi," Lizette replied, wondering at the quick friendliness. "You're up early."

"The guy I work for, he runs you day and night." The girl drew the squeegee down the window and wiped the blade. "Did your friend have a good time last night?"

"Wonderful," Lizette said without thinking.

"I was hopin' she would. She sure looked elegant."

Lizette stopped, her heart doing sudden flip-flops. "What friend?"

"Gosh, I dunno her name. The blondie. You an' her were both on duty in that do-it-yourself unit when I was in for X rays last spring. Always together, you two."

"And you saw her last night? *Here?*"

The girl nodded. "She said she was goin' out on a date."

"What on earth was she doing in the launderette?"

"She come for the suitcase. The woman sent her."

"The *woman* sent her?"

"Well, I dunno, I guess she said the woman couldn't come, I guess that was it. Anyways, she wanted the suitcase so I give it to her."

"What did it look like?"

"Kinda paper. Real light." The girl leaned on the handle of the squeegee. "Hey, was it hers all the time? Was she elopin' with the guy?"

"I really don't know."

"Listen, you all right? You look terrible."

"No, I — I'm just surprised. I never thought of her eloping."
Lizette hardly knew what she was saying. She must get to a
telephone, call Wakeley. "Did she say where she was going?"

"What's the good of runnin' away if you tell everybody?"

"That's right. And she was in a hurry, I suppose?"

"Oh, sure. Nervous, too. I sure hope the guy's good to her."

"He'd better be!"

The terrible conviction that the guy was not being good to
Jinny started Lizette on a run up the hill toward Waddy's
mortuary. The girl called after her, but she only waved her
hand. She had to reach Ted before he could leave for his date
with her. He would know what to do.

Her running steps carried her up the green matting and on
to the welcome mat. Panting, she pressed the bell. Soft chimes
sounded inside. She waited through an impatient minute. Then,
since the door remained closed, she tried the knob.

Afterward she would remember that the latch was not quite
caught. The door opened noiselessly. The hall was empty. Sunshine streamed through the windows of what was apparently a
drawing room and touched the first of the nice gray steps leading
upstairs.

"Ted?" Lizette inquired softly.

No answer. Judging from the very deep silence she was
the only living soul in the entire building. The only *living*
soul . . .

"Ted!" she called, but it was barely a whisper.

She could step back to the porch and keep pressing the bell
until someone came. But ahead, tucked in behind the stair well,
was a small doorway. The door stood open, showing light within
the little room. Probably an office.

Lizette went forward, her steps dropping noiselessly on the
gray carpet. She came into the little open door, and stopped.

Taking up most of the space was a casket, bronze finished,

lined with pale pink. In the casket Dannie lay. Ted had described her well. You couldn't believe, looking at her, that she had died by violence.

Why, she's beautiful, Lizette thought, and moved a little farther into the room. Several chairs had been placed facing the casket. There was a red plush prie-dieu, and at the foot of the casket on a pedestal was a marvelous pink cyclamen in full bloom. Together, these things took up most of the space.

But not all of it. On the carpet between the chairs and the dark drapery of the casket truck lay a man, face down, his gray curls partly hidden by the velvet folds. He was very still. Beside him a red stain had spread in an ugly blot.

Somebody began to scream, long piercing screams that hurt Lizette's head. She didn't realize they were her own until Ted rushed in, said something, and caught her to him. She began to cry then, hysterically, and she clung to him until he picked her up and carried her out into the big room where the sunshine was.

"All right now, take it easy, honey, take it easy," he kept saying, but his voice shook.

He put her into a big chair and began to rub her hands.

"Liz, darling, maybe there's something I can do for him, maybe he isn't . . . Calm down, will you, honey, so I can go?"

"Go where?"

"Just to the phone. I've got to call a doctor. I'll be right here in the hall."

"Wakeley! Get Wakeley."

"O.K., I'll call 'em both."

Lizette felt Ted pat her hastily on the head and collapsed sobbing against the chair arm. Mr. Waddy was dead. Like Jim McArthur. And Elizabeth. And Dannie Grear.

And Jinny?

"Oh, no, no, no!" Lizette sobbed into the chair arm.

Out in the hall she could hear Ted talking frantically to Wakeley. Today, tomorrow, some day the same kind of call would be made concerning Jinny because the man with the gruff voice had lured her away. He had told her to pick up the suitcase at the launderette. It was a dangerous mission. And now Jinny was missing in the place of her dearest friend, Lizette.

"I believe," Sister Simon said, tapping the scrapbook in her lap, "I firmly believe that the whole thing dates back to here. Henry Waddy was the link, you see. His death proves it."

Lizette shook her head slowly. The nun had sent for her and Diane, and the three of them sat on the screened porch of the Octagon House. They were going to sift back through what they knew for facts that would fit together, Sister Simon had said, through what was in the scrapbook and what Lizette had seen of Dannie on the water front and all that Diane remembered of her aunt. Somewhere there must be an answer to this terrible puzzle. But the bees were making lazy attempts to draw honey from the blossoms of the moonseed vine and their humming was like a sedative to Lizette.

"How does Mr. Waddy's death prove anything, Sister?" she asked, and her voice sounded far away, as it did in dreams.

"Someone must have been desperately afraid of what he might tell."

"Something about Aunt Dannie?" Diane asked incredulously. "Sister, if you think . . . you just don't understand what she was like . . . "

"Nothing personal, dear. But I'm absolutely convinced that she and Henry Waddy were killed for the same reason, because of something they knew."

"But what could it be?"

Diane was like a peevish child, pale and on the verge of

tears. We're all going to be like that, Lizette thought, if we don't stumble out of this quagmire pretty soon.

"They're all gone now," Sister Simon said, "all the men on the hunting trip, so we have to find another link if we can. Think hard, dear. Was there any friend, man or woman, about your aunt's age who might have known her through the past twenty years?"

"Nobody, Sister. Nobody except Mr. Barron."

"The lumberman? Vince Barron?" Lizette asked. "But he's . . . I mean . . . "

"He's a millionaire several times over. I know. And Aunt Dannie was poor as a church mouse. But he was her friend. He even came to see us quite regularly when I was small."

"But not lately?"

"How could I know that, Liz? I've been here at school."

"I wonder," the Sister said slowly. "I just wonder if he knows the same thing, whatever it might be, that Mr. Waddy knew, and Dannie."

Diane looked at her with wide eyes, started to speak, then suddenly jumped up and ran down the steps and away across the lawn. The two who remained on the porch watched her until she disappeared around a lilac bush.

"Sister," Lizette said after a moment, "Mr. Barron was a friend of Henry Waddy's. Ted mentioned him, what a strange sort of man he is. If he knows whatever this is, he could be the next victim."

"Yes. Or the murderer."

A bee worrying the last drop of nectar out of a moonseed blossom made a very loud buzzing. It seemed the most important thing in the world to Lizette that she wait until he had buzzed on to the next flower.

It took him a long time to finish.

"I'd like to go to see Mr. Barron," she said then. "I'd find out very casually where he was last night, because if he has an alibi so he couldn't possibly have had anything to do with Jinny's disappearance, or with Mr. Waddy's death, then he isn't the murderer. And he deserves a warning."

Sister Simon moved, easing herself in the chair. "He has an office, doesn't he, somewhere in town?"

"Straight over from the bank. You can see it, going to Waddy's."

"Well . . . then go in daylight, Lizette."

The girl smiled. "I'll be a student writing a term paper on the lumber industry, Sister. That ought to open him up. From what I've heard, it's been his whole life."

"Don't mention Dannie Grear. Or Virginia."

"I won't unless he does."

"Are you sure you want to do this, Lizette? You look so tired."

"I'll rest when I get back."

But there would be no rest for her until Jinny was found. Hurrying back to her room, changing her dress, giving her hair a dash with a comb, Lizette wondered how to begin her interview. A write-up for the school paper, perhaps that would be better. Still, how could she wind around to the vital question of where were you last night, Mr. Barron?

When she climbed the steps to the dismally bare house, Lizette was as fluttery as she had been on her first day in surgery. On the glass of the door in large gold letters was the name, "Barron Timberlands, Inc." Barron the millionaire, the little store clerk Dannie Grear, gentle Mr. Waddy, and young Jinny from the backwoods — how in the world could they all be linked together? And was the count three dead and one to go?

Lizette grasped the door latch and pushed. The hall was dim after the brilliant sunshine, but no amount of light could have made it cheerful. The walls were papered in brown oatmeal and in the corner was an ancient umbrella stand with a clouded mirror. A worn rubber runner led to a narrow stairs going up into more dimness. Nearest Lizette was a door with a beveled glass bearing the name, "V. W. Barron." There was darkness behind it. While she hesitated, wondering whether to knock, a door opened down the hall, seemed to be on the point of closing again, then swung barely wide enough to let a woman through. She was stocky and middle-aged, and she looked Lizette up and down, perhaps not with hostility but definitely taking her measure.

"Good afternoon," she said. She had a good voice and she was all competence, her hair cut like a man's, her blouse plain and very clean, and her shoes flat-heeled. Lizette felt frivolous in contrast. Mentally she stammered over the possible beginnings she had rehearsed on the way and found none of them adequate. Directness would be the best possible line with this person.

"I'd like to see Mr. Barron," she said. "If he isn't busy."

"Mr. Barron has not come in yet."

"Oh."

The only thing to do now was to leave. Or else state her business bluntly.

"I'm Lizette Carter, a student nurse at St. Matthew's. Diane McArthur is one of my friends." She paused, then since the woman showed no reaction she added, "Dannie Grear was Diane's aunt."

"I see."

It came casually enough, yet something changed in the woman's demeanor. She had not been smiling before, but now she looked as if she never had smiled in her life.

"And why did you wish to see Mr. Barron?"

Take the plunge, Lizette decided, get it over. "Diane said he was a friend of her aunt's, and I just thought . . . perhaps I should have come yesterday?"

"You'd have had to make it early. He's been gone since yesterday morning."

So Vince Barron was out of town when Jinny was lured away. He could have been the gruff voice on the telephone, but Tony would have known if it was a long-distance call. And if he had nothing to do with Jinny's disappearance, he wouldn't be involved in the death of Mr. Waddy, either.

"What is your business with Mr. Barron?"

"Sister Simon thinks — and so do I — that all this trouble about Dannie has come out of something that happened twenty years ago. And since Mr. Barron was a friend of hers, he may know whatever it was she was killed for, and so he may be in danger, too!"

It was an impulsive confidence. The moment she had finished, Lizette wondered whether she had been wise. But if the disclosure was startling, the secretary gave no indication. With a quick nod, she led the way back to the open door, stood aside for the girl to enter, and then, although the silence seemed to imply that they were alone in the building, she closed the door.

"Sit down," she said.

The room had most likely been one of the double parlors of the old home for a wide archway had been filled in with compoboard, and steel filing cabinets were ranged against it. On top of the cabinets were piled folders and papers of all kinds. More folders were stacked on a big square table. The desk behind which the woman seated herself was littered; but it was an orderly litter, and it occured to Lizette that this was the office of the executive rather than the other behind the darkened door.

"I'm Alice Armstrong," the woman stated. "I've been Mr. Barron's secretary for eighteen years. Now what's this about him being in danger?"

"We don't really know. The hunting party is the only . . . "

"What hunting party?"

"When Diane's father was killed. Jim McArthur. He and his brother Steve and Henry Waddy were deer hunting. It was an accident. Steve disappeared, afterward."

"And where does Dannie Grear come in?"

"She was a sister to Jim's wife, Elizabeth. Then when Elizabeth died in the fire only a short time later, Dannie took the baby, Diane, to raise her."

Lizette paused. Miss Armstrong was listening intently, her gaze on a glass bubble paperweight containing two cows in a barnyard.

"Dannie was a nun at the time of the fire," the girl continued. "She hadn't taken her final vows. She left in order to care for Diane."

"So that's why he gave them the house," Miss Armstrong said.

Lizette caught her breath. "The Octagon House? You mean Mr. Barron gave it to the Sisters when Dannie left?"

"When she entered. Twenty-two years ago." The secretary turned the paperweight upside down, then righted it, and watched the snow fall around the cows. "I found the record of it. I wondered why . . . he's not a specially charitable man . . . he wanted to think he provided a home for her, I suppose."

"But why?"

"You know the date today? August seventh. Every year on this day he'd go to visit her. Don't ask me why because I don't know . . . or do I?"

"You mean he was in love with her?"

"Why not?"

"From what I've heard of Mr. Barron, he wouldn't fall in love with anybody!"

"Nobody ever knows the why of loving someone, do they?"

Lizette fastened her gaze again on the cows. Was it possible that Miss Armstrong was in love with her boss? And Barron wouldn't even suspect it. He was too busy chasing after a woman who was so tangled up in something or other that she'd got herself murdered.

"He never mentioned Dannie Grear to me, naturally," the secretary added. "It's not a thing you'd discuss with somebody like him. Or me."

"Then how did you know about her?"

"A cousin of mine up in Beechwood Falls lived with Dannie for a while after Diane left to go to school. Nettie Julian. She's dead now." She picked up a pencil and drew a large X through the date on the calendar. "Who is this nun you mentioned?"

"Sister Simon. My supervisor."

"Is she doing some sleuthing on her own?"

"Not exactly. But Chief Wakeley doesn't feel that this business of the hunting accident has anything to do with Dannie and Mr. Waddy, and Sister Simon does. And since Mr. Barron was a friend of Dannie's . . . "

The secretary shoved away the calendar and rose. "I wouldn't worry about Mr. Barron. He can take care of himself. As for his friendship with Dannie Grear — well, he's paying her funeral expenses. Maybe if I stick with him long enough, he'll do the same for me, who knows?"

Lizette, letting herself out into the hot sunshine, thought hastily back over all the woman had told her. It wasn't evidence, exactly. The only real fact that emerged was the gift of the Octagon House to the Sisters, but Barron even in those days was a very rich man and the timing with Dannie's entrance into the convent might have been coincidence. According to Miss Armstrong, and Diane also, he had visited Dannie through the years. But it might not have been because he loved her. He could have been threatening her, too.

Down on the sidewalk, Lizette looked back up at the square, unlovely house. Barron was a good name for the man, that was what his life had been. And Miss Armstrong's must be barren, too. I wonder, Lizette thought, I wonder why I didn't mention Jinny to her? Quickly she turned away and hurried along the tree-shaded street.

Over on Main Street, Lizette turned left along the high walk which topped the retaining wall. People hung as usual against the railing, looking down on the park. She glanced toward the docks. The *Triton* was out. Ted would be declaiming the wonders of Stand Rock about now. On the portico of the Nickelodeon Palace the mind reader sat before his purple tent. He wore the garb of his profession, the white satin shirt and Paisley vest badly in need of cleaning, the orange turban dark with perspiration around the edges. The newspaper he held before him was a rather incongruous note. He should be gazing into a crystal ball. But he was not reading the newspaper, Lizette noted. He was looking past it, down at her.

She stopped. The man's eyes returned instantly to his paper. Merlin the mind reader had been present during that crucial time when Dannie had been so frightened down on the water front. And his client, Jinny, would certainly be known to him if he cared to remember her.

Rising, he stooped to pick up the stool on which he had been seated.

"Just a moment, please," Lizette said impulsively, and mounted the steps.

The mind reader paused, turning to her, his expression blank.

"I wonder if you'd remember the woman who was murdered? Dannie Grear? You were there that night, by the river."

He shook his head, the gold hoops dangling against his fat jowls. "I am seldom anywhere but here."

"Oh, but I saw you! You were on the stairs, and she was looking at the mud figures."

"I go many times to the park."

Lizette hesitated, wondering if she should remark the contradiction. "You must remember Dannie. She was so pathetic, lugging her suitcase. And frightened. Someone down there frightened her. I thought you might know who it was."

Merlin's eyes went to the stool he was folding. When an edge of canvas caught in the joint, he extracted it carefully.

"A mind reader does not glance over a crowd and read everyone's thoughts."

"But surely you remember her!"

"I see hundreds of people in a day."

Lizette was exasperated. He was not answering her questions at all, neither was he lying. She would try one more shot in the dark.

"Then you wouldn't remember my buddy, either. Jinny Johnson. She's come to you a couple of times this summer to have her palm read, but there's nothing remarkable about her. She's just — Jinny."

"Then why do you mention her?"

"Because she's missing."

Lizette thought later that she must have imagined the slight flare of alarm that crossed the man's face. He did not bother to reply. But it was with almost too much nonchalance that he proceeded into his tent. The first section was wide open, furnished with a dirty piece of carpet, a table holding a crystal ball, and two chairs. Inside, he raised another flap into an inner compartment, and Lizette had a glimpse of an unmade cot.

Slowly she went on down the long hill. The bridge had been built in the days of carriage traffic and the two lines of cars meeting one another nearly touched fenders. The sidewalk was too narrow for comfort. When the ambulance siren began to wail up on Main Street, Lizette hugged the rail. Even the ambulance could not pass swiftly here, and she had a good look into it as it went by. There was a sheeted figure on the stretcher and a white-coated attendant seated beside it. On the second seat was the woman Lizette had seen only minutes ago, Miss Alice Armstrong, who knew nothing of the whereabouts of her boss, which was strange, for the man on the stretcher could be none other than Vince Barron.

Chapter Twelve

SISTER JOE was not taking her customary pleasure in her little card game, and she was disappointed in herself. For years now, ever since she had educated Sister Jude to be her partner, she had looked forward to the recreation hour. Tonight, because the day had been so troubled, her anticipation had been even keener than usual. But something was wrong. She peered out over her spectacles at the assembled Sisters, thirty of them, all with lips moving in speech or laughter, all working at knitting or embroidery or jigsaw puzzles. The television was on, showing a pretty girl singing, but singing was just people opening their mouths when you couldn't hear. Sister Vitus was ripping her crocheting again, the same chalice design that Damian had been using for the altar cloth. . . .

Taking up the cards, Sister Joe began to shuffle them in long fans that appeared to rest in mid-air like a magician's trick. Frank had taught her to shuffle that way. It was he who had taught her to play cards back in the days when she had gone from one lumber camp to another collecting hospital insurance from the lumberjacks. With that money, St. Matthew's had made its beginning. Frank used to joke about it. Everything was funny to him. The sight of a nun dealing a poker hand was a huge joke. She never had played for money, of course, and never with anyone but Frank, her own brother. Those had been great days. Often, when the cook was sick or they were between cooks, she had turned in and fried the bacon. . . .

Sister Jude kicked her lightly under the table. Mother Richard had come in. Sister Joe lowered the cards to the conventional shuffle. Mother knew about the poker. She had participated once in a while before she had become superior, and she had been a reckless player. But now they all pretended she knew nothing about it. Not that there was a thing wrong with a game you played with buttons. Poker just sounded a little racy for a convent.

She dealt the cards expertly.

"Sweeten the pot, Sister."

She must have spoken too loudly because Sister Jude jumped and put her finger to her lips. The old nun's eyes went again around the circle. At times such as this she would have liked to hear, for Mother appeared to be telling something of high interest. Touching her thumb to her tongue, Sister Joe began to deal. Later, perhaps, someone would tell her the news. If not, she could offer the sacrifice of her curiosity for the poor souls.

"You open, Sister," she said.

The game began. But Sister Jude was so erratic in her playing it was difficult to tell what she meant, and finally she laid her cards face down on the table.

"Are you calling, Jude?" Sister Joe asked. "If you are, that's no way to go about it. Frank always said . . . "

"Sh!"

The old nun understood that well enough. She might as well gather up the buttons. Sister Jude's attention was gone from the game. Snapping the cover on the button box, she pushed back her chair and plodded out of the room and down the stairs. She was tired tonight. A half hour's reading in bed would send her off to sleep.

The lumberman had built his house well, but Sister Joe's tramp sent a shiver through half the cloister. The only light was a spare glimmer in the ceiling. All the doors were open upon oblongs of darkness. Except for one. In the third oblong from the end on the right there was a flash. Lightning? Sister Joe stopped. If she could feel the vibration of the thunder, then the storm was close and she would go back upstairs. Nothing happened. The light did not show again. Sister Edmond had sinus and was going to bed early, that was it. Everyone left her door open these hot nights. The old nun trudged forward. Perhaps Edmond would like some hot ginger tea.

The room, as she looked in, was dark but against the grayness of the window she could see that the plain white bed was unoccupied. The curtains, clipped neatly back with clothespins, left the window available for any passing breeze. There were no screens on these windows because the wide porch was tightly screened. Sister Joe grunted. Lightning, it must have been.

And then, just as she was turning away, a black blot began rising against the lightness of the window, cautiously, slowly widening into shoulders and an arm braced against the window frame.

"Who's there?" Sister Joe boomed.

The figure swayed. There was something eerie in the way it remained poised half above the sill, featureless, incredibly quiet. Then, for no apparent reason, it began to sink away.

"Who is it?" she demanded again.

If there was a reply, she did not hear it. Never in all the years she had been in the convent had there been an intruder; but this person must be one. If he had legitimate business, why did he not come openly to the door and ring the bell?

For a long minute the old nun remained still, listening so intently that her fingers were pressed to numbness against the door jamb. Even the black blot of the head had disappeared now. There was nothing to indicate anything unusual had happened except the tingling sensation running along her spine.

Shutting the door with a slam she could hear herself, Sister Joe lumbered down the hall and out into the lobby, turned back to dip her finger in the holy-water cup, started up the stairs, and walked into her habit as she had not done since she was a novice. Jerking the habit out of the way, she ascended at a speed that brought her panting into the recreation room.

"Mother!" she boomed, and everyone jumped to face her. She still held her scapular clutched up in a bundle and she folded her arms across it. "Mother, there's a burglar in the cloister! In Sister Edmond's cell! He came through the window!"

She might have added something about calling the police but the Sisters, having waited mere seconds for Mother to lead the way, were already pouring past. When Sister Joe again reached the landing, the long stairs was a waterfall of waving veils being rapidly siphoned off into the cloister.

She came in with the last trickle. The door she had closed now stood open. Mother had turned on the light. Nobody was under the bed. The closet held nothing but Sister Edmond's other habit and her winter cloak and rubbers. The only proof that an intruder ever had been there was a dark smudge on the wall under the window.

"I don't wonder he's gone," Sister Joe observed. "He wouldn't stand around waiting to be caught."

No one answered her. Vaguely she could catch the word police. Mother was going to call them. It was the proper step. But they wouldn't find him. There had been so much trouble over Damian, perhaps this was part and parcel of it all.

Sister Joe went into her own cell and closed the door. Things she would just as soon remember were completely gone out of her head, but Damian's letter haunted her. She couldn't even forget where she had put it. Pushing aside the curtain of her closet, she looked up at the shelf. There it was, her new forgetting book, *Uranium Prospecting in Northern Minnesota.* She wouldn't take it down tonight. And possibly by morning she would have forgotten the letter.

Seating herself in her rocker, she took out her rosary.

Sister Simon came into the Octagon House just as Mother Richard hung up the telephone after calling the police. A prowler, the nuns babbled excitedly, had been in the cloister and goodness knew what might have happened if Sister Joe hadn't discovered him.

"There's even fingerprints on the wall!" young Sister Pius twittered. "Come and see!"

"We don't know why he'd want to get into the cloister," said Sister Jude. "We've never had a burglar before!"

"He could have mistaken it for the nurses' home," Sister Pius suggested, "only what would he be after there, either? He ought to know the girls don't have any money!"

"It wouldn't be money," Sister Simon murmured, already on her way out. The prowler could very well have mistaken the Octagon House for the nurses' home.

Out in the dark, the Sister began to run. Vince Barron had been admitted to the hospital this afternoon, unconscious from a bad concussion. The ambulance siren had barely sighed into nothing when Lizette, returned from her errand, had come hurrying up to pedes with a nervous account of a strange interview with a secretary who insisted Mr. Barron was out of town and yet a few minutes later was seen accompanying him in the ambulance, and of a second disturbing little conversation with Merlin the mind reader. Jinny was gone. And now Lizette?

Sister Simon was panting like a long-distance sprinter when she threw open the door to Lizette's room. Over by the window, in the dark, someone was seated. She snapped the light switch. In the sudden brightness Lizette blinked, then turned to bury her face in her arms on the sill.

"Sorry, dear," the Sister said, and flipped the switch again. "We'll have the lamp on instead. Why are you sitting here in the dark?"

"I'm thinking."

Turning on the small study lamp, Sister Simon glanced immediately at the window screen beyond Lizette. It was intact. He could have reached her so easily, sitting there. . . .

"What are you thinking about, Lizette?" the nun asked casually.

Lizette, still resting her head on her arms, faced the Sister. She was as pale as Diane had been in the afternoon, with the same drawn look, her dark eyes too big.

"I was thinking how unfair life is, Sister. Awful things happen to other people, but for me everything is perfect. I get along in school, I have a wonderful boy friend, my folks are so good to me — but look at Jinny! She had a miserable life at home. Even if she graduates she'll be a terrible nurse, we all know that. The only bright spot was being Blueberry Queen. . . ."

She stopped, hiding her face again.

Sister Simon looked around the room. All of Jinny's clutter had been cleared away, her bed smoothly made, her stuffed rooster rakishly perched on the pillow. Deliberately the Sister sat down on that smooth bed and caught at the spread to wrinkle it a little.

"The only answer I can give you, Lizette, is that we aren't in a position to judge the fairness of life. There's an old story, you must have heard it, about a man who stood watching a nun scrubbing a floor, and he said, 'Sister, I wouldn't lead your kind of life for a million dollars.' And she smiled and said, 'Neither would I.' The purpose is what counts, you see. Jinny feels that she is really getting somewhere, she's not a bit sorry for herself. And there's a place for her in nursing. Couldn't you imagine what a comfort she would be to a bedridden old lady?"

Lizette straightened, smiling through tears. "What a dear thing to think of, Sister."

"Much more will be expected of you. So take your happiness and be thankful for it."

"Oh, I always am! Like yesterday morning. Ted and I had such a perfect time on our picnic up in the Gorge. A little boy came along with a rusty old gun over his shoulder and had breakfast with us. Ted told him the gun had undoubtedly belonged to Wyatt Earp, he even pretended he could see the initials on the stock, W E instead of W L. . . ." She paused, frowning. "That's been bothering me, Sister. Why should W L ring a bell?"

"It does with me, too. I seem to see it in print. What have I been reading lately? Sister Joe's old scrapbook?"

"That's it, Sister! Remember, right at the end of the clipping, it mentioned the other hunter who was missing, besides Steve McArthur? Willis Lawrence!"

"Where did the boy get the gun?"

"He said he found it in the river."

"Do you know his name?"

"No. Ted called him Jim Bowie. And the initials are changed now because Ted made the L into an E. For Wyatt Earp." Lizette rose, to lean on the end of the bed. "Sister, could this have any connection with the hunting accident?"

"I don't see how it could." But the nun spoke as if the breath had been knocked out of her. "No, of course not. Willis wasn't hunting with Henry Waddy's party. How could there be a connection?"

She was protesting too much, she well knew. But she couldn't look squarely at the terrifying possibility that had popped full fledged into her mind.

"You're thinking of something, Sister," Lizette accused her. "Something you're not going to tell me."

"Are you trying to be a mind reader, too, dear?" Sister Simon looked at her watch. "Nine o'clock. You can sleep for at least an hour and a half before you go on duty. And you should do it, Liz, you look tired."

"All right, Sister, I'll try."

The girl was puzzled and not quite pleased, the nun reflected as she hurried away. But far better to leave her that way than with nebulous imaginings. The only certain sure fact was that Willis had lost his gun.

The Sister, however, fled through the alley at such a pace that her stiff skirts made a clatter in the echoing old place. In the convent the Great Silence had begun and there was no sound except a few footsteps. There would be no more conversation until breakfast time. Sister Simon went straight to her cell and took the scrapbook from a drawer in her writing desk. Turning quickly to the page she had perused so often in the past hours, she ran her finger down to the bottom of the clipping. There it was, Willis Lawrence was missing. He had been on a deer hunting expedition with several people, among them his brother Bartholomew.

Returning to the hall, the Sister closed the cloister door tightly behind her. No one would hear her using the phone. There were several Lawrences listed in the telephone book, two of them Bartholomew, father and son because one of them was Junior. She dialed Senior.

Her heart thudded as she listened to the ringing, one, two, three — and the line opened.

"Hello," a woman's voice said.

"May I speak to Mr. Bartholomew Lawrence, please?"

"Just a moment."

Now what in the world would she say? She should have taken a few minutes to think this out carefully.

"Mr. Lawrence speaking," a man said into her ear.

"I'd like to get in touch with Willis Lawrence," Sister Simon told him. "I understand he's your brother."

There was a small hesitation. "Willis disappeared twenty years ago. We never knew what became of him. What did you want to get in touch with him for?"

Sister Simon would have given anything in the world if she could have dropped the telephone like the teen-agers who make bother calls and hang up as soon as you answer; because there was someone coming quietly through the long corridor from the front door, and the tread was unmistakably Mother Richard's.

"I believe something belonging to Willis has been found," Sister Simon said hurriedly. "I'll call you tomorrow morning. Good-by."

She did drop the receiver then. Poor Bartholomew, he would lie awake wondering who owned this voice out of the past; but she couldn't explain about a gun, not with Mother crossing herself at the cloister door, waiting for her. She should not have called Bartholomew in the first place; but Chief Wakeley would make light of this new clue, if such it could be called, and besides there was still her own lingering sense of guilt concerning Dannie's cry for help which she had not permitted to be answered. She couldn't dwell on her doubts, especially to a person who never had been mentally tousled herself. Mother would simply repeat her reassurances. Leave murder to the police. For yourself, sift the facts sensibly and you will see you

did right, then forget it. With only a nod, so as not to break
the Silence, Sister Simon followed Mother into the cloister.

In her own cell with the door closed, she could not shut off
the terrible conclusion that was not merely a hunch any more.
The facts were too indisputable. Willis Lawrence had not returned because he was dead. His gun had been found in the
river. A skeleton, presumably that of Steve McArthur, was discovered in a ravine some years later, but the only identification
was superficial, a watch with Steve's initials. The watch
belonged to Steve. He had put it where it was discovered —
on Willis Lawrence's wrist.

Slowly the nun walked over to the desk and gazed down
at the clipping. Jim had died, Elizabeth had died — not by
accident, either of them. Dannie had known that their deaths
had not been accidental. Henry Waddy knew it. Vince Barron
could be suspected of knowing and so an attempt had been
made on his life. There was only one answer: Steve had come
back. And the awful chain twenty years long would not be
broken until he was found.

With the musket against his shoulder, Eddie skulked rapidly
up the Witches' Gorge. He had to do his skulking rapidly because it would soon be dark and he was not supposed to be
here at all. His mother had finally put her foot down. It was
his own fault, in a way, because yesterday morning he had
forgotten all about the time, with Ted carving the initial on
the gun and telling stories about Wyatt Earp, and it was long
past noon when Eddie got home. Mom had been worried sick.
Anything could happen, she said, out in those hideous ravines.
He could fall down a cliff and lie there with a broken leg until
he died, she said, and all they'd ever find would be his bones.
It was the end, she said, to the kid running wild. So now he
would have to do his skulking when she didn't know about it,

and this evening was his first chance. His mother and dad were gone somewhere, and Janet was on the front porch with her goony boy friend and not caring a bit what her little brother did as long as he kept out of sight. And hearing. There was just about time for a quick trip through the Gorge.

It would be great, Eddie thought, if he could dally along until the last bunch of settlers came through the draw and say hello to Ted. Only he wasn't sure that Ted would be the guide, and he didn't dare stay away long enough to be missed. He'd better just bring down a few squirrels and head for home. Crouching on one knee, he sighted along the lofty top of the ravine. Nothing moved but a few ferns away up against the sky. His thumb rubbed softly at the initials on the stock of the gun. He'd thought so much about Wyatt Earp, after Ted's stories, that it almost seemed as if the weapon had really belonged to the famous frontiersman. It sure was a dandy shootin' iron.

Down the ravine behind him, Eddie heard a woman's high-pitched laugh. Settlers. Or Indians. He hadn't expected them in this neck of the woods. Hide, that's what Wyatt would do, until he'd see whether this was friend or enemy. Up ahead, just beyond the narrow turn they called Fat Man's Misery, was the old glacial cell he had explored the other day. Duck in there and he'd be safe. He could even pick off a few Indians as they filed by.

Laying the gun on the sidewalk, Eddie swung under the railing, took up the gun again, and on his knees backed into the circular cavity in the rock. It was a lot bigger than he'd thought before. There was a lip coming down and partly blocking the entrance; but right inside, the ceiling was nearly high enough so he could stand upright. Toward the back it curved down like an igloo, with a rounded wall. . . .

Eddie, pivoting on his knees, was suddenly motionless. He

was not alone in the cell. A girl lay with her back against the wall, sound asleep. Out in the draw, the woman settler laughed again.

Lizette had turned off the light and lain down, but there was no way to turn off her thoughts. Staring up at the shadowy ceiling, she could see Sister Simon's pretty face, bewildered, even a little frightened. Exactly what the nun was thinking she could not quite deduce, for her head felt like a musty attic jammed full of the remains of things; but one fact she did know for sure: Sister's sudden brain wave had been inspired by the gun. The gun which had belonged to Willis Lawrence.

Lizette sat up, battered her pillow into another shape, and lay down again. She was not going to be shut out of making any discovery that could possibly help either to find Jinny or to throw light on the situation concerning Dannie and Henry Waddy. One obvious contribution would be to find the gun. She could do that very easily. At eleven she would go on duty, and Ted would have returned to the mortuary. She would call him and suggest another picnic up the Gorge in the morning. He'd agree, for he was more than ready to do anything she wished, these days. Jim Bowie had had such a good time yesterday morning with them that there was more than a possibility he would happen along again. And if he shouldn't come, Ted would think of a way to get in touch with him. Then they would borrow the gun. Sister Simon — or the police — could take it from there.

Sighing heavily, she closed her eyes.

Eddie watched the girl for a full minute. She was a real pretty girl. She had blond hair and it was fanned out over the dark rock, and her dress was about the color of Mom's lilacs last spring. Eddie didn't know whether he should wake her up or not. She certainly couldn't be very warm in this damp room. She'd catch her death of cold, lying there like that with no coat on.

"Hello," he said. The girl didn't move, so he said it louder. "Hello!" Still she didn't wake up. He inched over on his knees and touched her shoulder. It felt ice cold through the thin dress.

"Hey, listen, you're gonna get pneumonia," Eddie told her, and he gave her shoulder a small push against the wall. She rolled back a little but her arm, bent to lie along the rock, stayed in the same stiff position and on her dress, where her hand had been, there was a dark brown stain. Like the stain on the bandage when he'd cut his thumb so bad with the hatchet.

Eddie snatched back his hand. He had seen only one dead person — Grandpa, and he had looked like he was alive in his casket, only better. He suddenly was very sorry for this girl. Nobody would say like they did about Grandpa that it was a blessing she was gone, she had suffered so much. She was so pretty she ought to be alive. And somebody grown up had to come, not just a kid.

He scuffled over to the opening. The settlers were right at the curve. He could hear the guide explaining about the glacier, but it wasn't Ted's voice. While Eddie hesitated, other feet began to go by, girls' and men's and everything. And then a cautious thought struck him. He was not supposed to be here in the Witches' Gorge. Let him tell those people there was a dead girl in the cell and they'd never just say thanks, go on home now. They'd ask what's your name, how did you find her, where do you live, and his folks couldn't help hearing about it. Then he'd sure have some tall explaining to do. He could have trusted Ted. Ted would have worked out something to save his skin. As it was, he sure was in a pickle.

Shivering, his knees icy as the girl's shoulder on the cold rock, Eddie crouched in the dimness while the feet filed by. He didn't know what to do. It didn't seem right just to go off and leave the girl because nobody else would go diving into this place and she'd never be found. Nothing would hurt her, though, because animals didn't come down here from the forest above, there was nothing to eat for them, Ted had said so. Gol-*lee*, why hadn't he stayed home tonight and maybe crawled around under the porch and listened to Janet and the boy friend if he'd wanted something to do? Only Mom had made him promise never to do that again after the time he'd choked with laughing and given himself away.

Eddie drew a long, trembling breath and hugged the gun. If he could figure out what Wyatt Earp would do in this case, maybe that would be the answer. Of course things were a lot simpler for Wyatt, not having folks to demand where in the world were you. Still, for other reasons he had to do things on the q.t., like when he was chasing outlaws and didn't want them to get wise to the fact that they were being trailed. If he'd discovered the girl while he was on a ride like that, and couldn't let anyone know he'd found her, he'd — well, wouldn't he lead somebody else to do the discovering all over again?

"You betcha!" Eddie whispered aloud. "You just betcha!"

The whole scheme fairly blasted out of his head. He had a beat up old crayon in his pocket. All he needed was a piece of paper, and he knew where to find one. The only chancy part was that he'd have to be out a little later than he'd planned, but Mom was going to mark up a hem for Aunt Margaret and that always led to more sewing talk, and Janet would be so glad he wasn't pestering that she'd never think of stirring him up by looking in his room. He'd be safe for quite a while yet.

The last of the feet went by and the voices drifted out of

hearing, up the draw. The settlers wouldn't be coming back for a while, plenty long enough for what Eddie had to do. Scrambling out, he piled loose rocks in the open archway. The girl would be protected, and the rocks would be a landmark for Ted, doing the discovering. Then all he'd have to do would be to get the paper, write the note, a thought which sorta frightened him because he wasn't any good at spelling, and wait for the boat to depart from the landing at the foot of the Gorge. The waiting was so the wrong guy wouldn't get the note. It had to be Ted. And Ted, he knew from experience, would be the first guide up here tomorrow afternoon. He'd be sure to see the note, where Eddie would stick it.

He almost whistled as he ran down the sidewalk. Things were mighty easy when you worked them out like Wyatt Earp.

Chapter Thirteen

AT ONE O' CLOCK in the morning the water front was as quiet as it would ever be. The jukeboxes had stopped their blaring, the skates were all hung up in the roller rink and the rifles racked in the shooting gallery. Except for a big semitruck rolling down the hill to the bridge, Main Street was clear of traffic. The man trudged along the high sidewalk, his head down. Without the orange turban and in baggy tans, he was an inconspicuous figure. At the top of the boat company's fine stairs he glanced quickly up and down the street, then let himself down a careful step at a time to the riverside park. Cutting across the brown sod to the cluster of trailers, he went straight to a small, weatherbeaten one, knocked, and without waiting tried the door. It did not open. A fierce barking began inside, a voice swore, and the barking subsided to a growl.

The mind reader put his face close to the keyhole. "It's Smith. Let me in."

The voice swore again and muttered something about the middle of the night, but there was the creak of a bedspring and in a few moments the sound of a key turning in the lock. The man didn't wait for the door to open. Pushing hard, he slipped inside. The dog went into a fit of growling.

"Shut up, Barker!" Merlin snapped. "Lou, turn on a light before he takes a chunk out of me. Who does he think I am, a cop?"

"You never know."

The light switch clicked. Even with her hair combed, Lou Tobias couldn't be called a good-looking woman. Routed out of bed, without the heavy make-up and in a crumpled housecoat, she was a hard-favored sight. Along her jaws was a stubble equal to Merlin's.

The mind reader tramped across to the davenport. Lou's trailer always looked as if she were having a rummage sale. Pushing aside some magazines and a bread wrapper, he sat down. He hated to say what he had to say, but after all it was what he had come for.

"I made a mistake tonight, Lou."

"What's different about that?"

He drew his sleeve across his forehead and looked at the dark streak. "I went out to the hospital."

"What for?"

"The girl. She's getting too close."

"And what were you going to do about it, Smith?"

"It was Pico's idea, not mine. Scare the daylights out of her, put her off snooping. But I . . ." He shrugged broadly. "Well, I picked the wrong place."

"How do you mean you picked the wrong place?"

Merlin's eyes went clear around the trailer, over the dingy bed, the sink filled with bottles, the cluttered table, and down to Lou's bare feet.

"I got into the convent and some old nosey caught me at it."

The dog had lain down and was licking a paw. Merlin watched him because he dared not look up at Lou. With a wide sweep of her arm she cleared a space on the table. A can of milk bounced to the floor and rolled, leaving a white path behind it. Barker stretched his neck to lick at the milk. Lou swung one leg up to half sit on the table.

"So you got into the convent," she said in a venomously soft tone. "You know what happens now? Now they'll put a cop there day and night. I told you we'd get around to her, but you can't wait! No, you gotta act, quick like an elephant, clumsy, stupid . . ."

Merlin spread his hands helplessly. "She was asking if I remembered the woman. Dannie Grear, Lou!"

"Well, what of it? You were there. So was I. So was Pico. So were a hundred other people. If you keep your head, we're all right."

"I had to do something!"

Lou, swearing quietly, dug a cigarette pack out of the mess on the table. "I run the shooting gallery open and above board, I make a production out of being respectable, I don't get in trouble with the cops, ever — and what happens? I'm in trouble up to my neck!"

"Not yet, Lou."

"What you mean, not yet?"

"Wakeley was here, he went away, didn't he?"

"He'll be back. He said we're all kind of a brotherhood, us carnies, we show up in the same places year after year, follow a route north in the summer, south in the winter. We'd stick together, he said."

Merlin gave a sour laugh. "How long would we stick together if we didn't have something on each other? Brotherhood, my eye!"

"Wakeley ain't a fool." Lou turned cold eyes on her visitor. "And mother's little helper, here, he comes along to make things double easy for the cop. You a mind reader? If you were worth your weight in garbage you'd still be a no-count bum!"

The dog leaped up, growling. There had been no knock but

the doorknob turned. Almost with the turning the mud artist swung into the trailer. Lou showed no surprise. Barker went back to licking at the milk. The newcomer did not look as if he had been asleep. He glanced at Merlin.

"Oh, you," he said. "I saw the light. What's up?"

"More of same," Lou replied bitterly. "I'm sick of it."

"Too bad."

"It ain't grim enough we got cops diggin' around, this sharpie here, he's gotta crawl in the convent window!"

Pico threw back his head, roaring with laughter. "You're drinking the wrong brand again, Smith."

"What *you* laughing for?" Lou demanded.

Pico's face darkened. "I'll laugh whenever I feel like it, and don't you forget it," he said quietly. Going to the sink, he began to upend bottles, tossing them in the direction of the trash box when he found them empty. Lou watched him in sullen silence. Merlin drew his tongue across his lips. It would have been so much better if he hadn't come here, he could see that now. He hated to be near Pico. What if the fellow did hold the whip hand, he didn't have to be so brazen about it as he'd been lately.

"You and me, we're gonna have a talk pretty soon, Junior," Lou told Pico.

"What about?"

"Facts of life."

"Not interested."

"No?"

Lou jerked an empty sardine can toward her and ground out the cigarette. Going down on her knees, she shoved aside Merlin's feet, groped under the davenport, brought out a small, shabby suitcase and tossed it up on the pile of magazines. A sick trembling ran through Merlin. There was very little room for both him and the suitcase, and he drew away until he did not touch it. Lou sat back on her heels.

"Interested yet, Pico?"

He gave an insolent shrug. "That's your baby."

"What if I'm all through doing the dirty work?"

"Then I'd be ready to discuss the facts of life. Jailbreaks, for instance."

Lou's face turned beet red and she began to lumber to her feet, tripping on the housecoat. Merlin had been present during some of their brawls and he had no stomach for another. Squeezing past Lou, he brushed the sardine can off the table and stepped on Barker's paw; but he made it to the door and out. He'd certainly never talk to Pico like that, get him all riled up. Live and let live. Only things were certainly getting more complicated than they'd been in the beginning. . . .

Wiping his forehead, Merlin stood listening for the yelling to begin; but there were only a few gutturally vehement remarks and then silence. His nerves reached like antennae toward the trailer window. The sash was pushed out to let in air and there was a screen covered with a sagging curtain. He could see over the curtain if he could climb that high.

In the dark, being very quiet, he rummaged around until he found a washtub and a box. Turning the tub wrong side up, he set the box on top and mounted his perch. By stretching, he could see into the trailer.

The davenport was immediately under the window. Lou, facing Merlin, had opened the suitcase and was bent over it. Pico lounged against the sink, lazily lighting a cigarette, his beard like a shadow across his face. Merlin wanted to see what Lou was doing. He raised himself on tiptoe. Lou, bending over the suitcase, had let go of the housecoat and the front bagged open to the waist. The bare torso it disclosed was that of a man.

Merlin let himself down to the tub and then to the ground. He was always revolted somehow by any reminder that Lou merely pretended to be a woman. Good reason for a disguise, of course. Nobody would choose to go back to jail. But why not keep his male identity and go off to Siam or the North Pole?

Trudging away, Merlin tried to bring some sort of order out of his rattled thoughts. He was so keen at solving other people's problems, why not his own? He had tried, tonight. All he had accomplished was to arouse a conventful of women and make himself a laughingstock for Lou and Pico.

The river, at half past seven in the morning, was more quiet than it had been even in pioneer days. Then the still depths were rocky, murderous rapids where lumberjacks lost their lives breaking log jams and Indian canoes were caught in the eddies and whirled to pieces. Now in the great backwater above the dam there was only the tiny splash of oars as Ted rowed along. The swallows, although they appeared to be numbered in the thousands, made no slightest sound as they swooped low over the water after bugs or winged back to the cliffs honeycombed with their nests.

"You'd wonder how they all know which hole is theirs," Lizette said. "Do you suppose they ever get mixed up?"

"And feed the neighbors' wife and kiddies by mistake? I doubt it," Ted answered. "Instinct is a pretty trusty commodity."

"Instinct such as the birds have, maybe. Not ours."

"Like what?"

"Like self-preservation. That's what keeps our murderer going. He's killing now to protect himself."

"Could be. But you can't attribute killing to an instinct. That's using his intelligence, and he's gone berserk."

"Ted, if he's killed Jinny . . ."

"Let's not cross that bridge yet, honey."

Lizette trailed her fingers in the cool water. It was a shame to spoil the morning with talk of murder. But all night long she had run to listen every time Poppy answered the phone, hoping it was some word about Jinny, but none had come. She wasn't doing much, going after Jim Bowie and his gun, but it was better than nothing. Today would *have* to bring something in the way of a solution to Jinny's disappearance, it just wasn't possible to go on and on, waiting. Today, up in Marshlands, they would be having the Blueberry Festival. Without Jinny.

The little boat rounded a bluff and slid up beside the dock where the excursion boats stopped for the trip up the Witches' Gorge. Ted threw a rope around a post and tied it firmly. Then, with one foot in the boat and the other on the dock, he held out a hand to Lizette.

"Come on, lady. All ashore that's going ashore."

Lizette stepped out beside him. Above them, on top of the bluff, was the barny structure where the tourists bought coffee and postcards, its shutters closed at this early hour. A narrow path led past the flight of steps and immediately into the Gorge, the entrance used by all the guides. Starting along it, Lizette came to a sudden stop. In the middle of the path lay a small rock, and from under the rock protruded a folded piece of paper.

"What in the world . . . " she said, and stooped to push aside the stone. "Ted, it's a map. And it has your name on it!"

The lettering was done in crayon, "Ted," with a very crooked E.

"Some kid. Let's see, Liz."

The map was the printed sketch of the river and the tributary gorges which was given away free up above in the coffee shop. There was usually a box of the maps outside the door. A note was written in crayon on the back.

"Dont say nothing becas I am not spose to be here but I found a girl she is in the cave with the rocks pilled up good. You look and see. A frend."

Lizette read the note over Ted's elbow.

"Ted, what cave? *Is it Jinny?*"

His hand had fallen flat on the writing, crumpling it into a ball. "Liz, now let's not go off the deep end. This could be just a . . . a joke. You stay here and I'll . . . Liz, come back!"

But Lizette was already off at a staggering run up the narrow sidewalk leading into the Gorge. She could hear herself sobbing in the same way she had heard herself screaming when she found Henry Waddy, almost as if it were someone else making the noise. Slamming into the railing where it turned suddenly, she slid her palm along it and felt slivers piercing in. There were no rocks piled up here, no cave, nothing out of the ordinary except the chill dampness that always seemed odd on a summer day because it made you see your breath in steam. She could hear Ted behind her, begging her to stop. Once he caught hold of her but she pulled away. Squeezing through the Fat Man's Misery, she bumped her head on an outcropping and the sharp pain was like a stimulant to push her along. It couldn't be far now to the end of the ravine. If someone had played a cruel joke they would soon know. . . .

"Ted!" she screamed, "there it is! The rocks . . . the rocks . . ."

Lizette threw herself between the railing slats and began to tear at the stones, breaking her fingernails, bruising her hands. It was not a joke. The girl was in the cave, the girl who would have to be Jinny. . . .

"Darling, let me," Ted urged, trying to be calm; but he sent the rocks rolling. Daylight filtered past into the glacial cell. In the dimness, a little grayer than Lizette had seen it before, lay a fold of the orchid dress.

The small boat floated downstream so close to the riverbank that at times it struck a willow root and careened sideways.

Merlin, trying to keep from being dumped by the swift current, swore softly to himself. He was no riverman. He should have stayed ashore, walked, hitchhiked, anything but this. Only he had to do something inconspicuous, and the boat had seemed like the ready solution. It was the same boat in which the girl and Ted had made their hasty return from some expedition up in the other direction. Merlin, prowling restlessly through the back quarters of the Nickelodeon Palace, had seen their almost frantic landing, Ted's fumbling with the painter, the girl's rush away from him toward the stairs. He didn't know, then, what it meant. Later, he did. Pushing out his lower lip he blew, trying to cool his face. It didn't help.

He peered ahead through the willows. Other than to put as much distance as possible between himself and Wakeley, he hadn't thought of any particular destination when he started out, but the ghost town would do as well as anything. It had to be along here somewhere. The journey already had felt like fifty miles, so it must be at least two. The current slammed the boat against a protruding stump, yanked it free, and shot it around the bend. There, straight ahead, were the remains of a rickety old dock.

Merlin dug the oars deep. The boat, for once, went where he intended and came up with a whack against the pilings. He climbed out thankfully.

He had the boat tied before he remembered that anyone coming down the river, hunting him, would surely see the craft. Turn it loose and let it drift away — but he might need it again. Pull it up into the willows, that would be safe. Getting the heavy boat into the underbrush was hard work for his soft muscles, and his tan shirt was dark down the back before the task was done to his liking. He had to sit down then on the dock, for his heart was thudding as if it would burst. He must decide, before it was too late to go back, whether absence was a good idea. The empty tent would naturally draw Wakeley's attention. But flight didn't have to be an indication of guilt. It could mean you merely wanted to get away and think things over, get the proper perspective. Well, get it quick.

Merlin wiped his face, stood up, and peeled off his shirt. Dipping it in the water, he wrung it out and put it on again. But there was no real defense against the muggy heat. The cool morning had become sultry by noon, and now in early afternoon the sky was overcast and yellow, seeming to cup the heat down against the earth. Puffing hugely, he trudged up through the wide-open space between the willows and came into the ghost town.

Empty houses showed windows empty of glass and doors hanging by one hinge. The place had never been very big. There was supposed to be a sawmill somewhere. Coming to the first house he sat down in the gaping doorway and stared at the ground in front of him.

They had found the girl. He had hoped it wouldn't be so soon. Exactly how the discovery had come about he didn't know, but the young snooper from the hospital and the guide had made it. That was one of the things he had heard Wakeley throwing at Lou, back there in the trailer. Lord, if he'd walked in on Lou as he had had every intention of doing, there would have been the two of them in jail now, not just Lou. Merlin began to shake again as he had when he cowered outside the trailer, listening. Lou had stayed too long in the housecoat, for Wakeley had torn off the disguise. You could tell, from the things he said. And then he searched the trailer, not very far, either, because he came on the suitcase right away. Merlin squirmed out of the wet shirt. It didn't feel good any more. He couldn't sit still. Lumbering to his feet, the shirt dragging from one hand, he started up the desolate, dusty expanse that used to be Main Street. Homely weeds sprangled where people had walked. Some of them must have had problems. But not like his. For the first time in years he wondered if the new life he had taken on shouldn't have been something safe. Like plumbing. Mind readers found out things. It was an occupational hazard, in a way, that people would sometimes think you'd found out far more than you had. They never stopped to realize that their behavior broadcast their state of mind to anyone who observed them keenly. Fear, for instance. Fear was unmistakably easy to read. . . .

In the middle of the street, among ragweed waist high, Merlin stopped and looked around. Where was he going? There was no refuge here. Nothing to eat, either. An ancient sign that said "Cafe." lay on the ground, face up to the sky like a dead man. He looked back to where the willows half hid the dock. No refuge anywhere. And no return. Would he starve to death in this God-forsaken place?

"Merlin the Magnificent," he said aloud.

A small garter snake slipped out of the ragweed, flashed its forked tongue at him, and glided on. In the whole wretched town, he and the snake appeared to be the only things alive.

As he stood there, a raindrop hit him on the head.

Sister Simon stood at the foot of Vince Barron's bed and watched the man's uneasy, jerking movements.

"He's been doing that for the last hour," the special nurse said. "I haven't telephoned Wakeley. He said to let him know the minute Mr. Barron came around, but there's no use yet."

"He hasn't spoken?"

"No, you know how they do, Sister, coming out of a concussion. You'd think they were wrestling the whole human race. Maybe he's fighting off his assailant. He could have passed out, fighting, and he's just carrying on from there."

"It's possible," said the nun. "Of course, for him there has been no interval of lying here in the hospital. They don't know how this happened, do they?"

"I guess not, Sister. The secretary said she didn't go into his office until after noon, and then she thought he had come in while she was out to lunch and gone to sleep. Something he never did before. He's hardly the type for afternoon naps."

"But she didn't see anything wrong with him?"

"No. And there's very little mark on his head. The blow must have been made with a flat weapon of some kind."

"If it came from behind, he wouldn't know who hit him."

"Not even what, Sister." The nurse straightened the already straight sheet. She was a stout white-haired woman, handsome in her white uniform. "Well, Wakeley's hoping for some scrap of a clue. This is really a crazy, mixed-up mess, isn't it, Sister? Finding that poor kid up the ravine, honestly, you wonder who's next."

Sister Simon left, walked down all the stairs and out across the alley to the nurses' home. The answer to the question of who's next was almost too obvious. Everyone who knew Steve from the old days had been put out of the way. The only remaining threat was the girl who had seen him on the water front. But she couldn't know him as Steve! If only there was some way to reassure him! He hadn't waited, before, to have his fears quieted. He had struck, brutally and finally. Three times. Four, counting Vince Barron. Would it be five before the total could be counted?

The Sister tapped on Lizette's door, heard a faint answer, and entered. The girl sat in the little rocker, a notebook open on her lap. Rain was pelting in the window, making inky puddles out of the writing on the open pages.

"You're getting all wet, dear," Sister Simon said, and went quickly to close the window.

Lizette touched her own arm, then looked at her fingers as if she were surprised to find them wet.

"It's not a very good day for the Blueberry Festival, is it, Sister?"

The nun had to swallow hard before she could reply. "Just a shower, I expect. Where can I find a towel?"

"Jinny has a clean one. On the back of the closet door."

They didn't talk while Sister Simon dried Lizette's arm and dabbed up the water on the floor. All the odds and ends of Jinny's life were still around, like the clean towel she hadn't had a chance to use. Her stuffed rooster was perched on the pillow, a brush with a few blond hairs on the dresser, in the wastebasket the face tissues she had probably used, her clothes still in the closet. But her folks were on their way to town and they would take the little physical things that remained of Jinny, and every trace of her would be blotted away like the puddle from the floor. But Jinny was only an element of a greater entity. Sorrow for her must not obliterate the real concern, which must be for the girl who sat like a rag doll in the rocker.

Sister Simon dropped the wet towel beside the door and returned to stand before Lizette. She didn't quite know how to begin because she had no real idea of what she wanted to say. A policeman had brought Lizette home this morning because Ted was needed to lead the rescue party up the Gorge, and Dr. Barney had given her a sedative. Even with that, she had not slept well, Sybil reported, and the grogginess still persisted. Mother Richard had done the only sensible thing in telephoning Lizette's parents. And yet, if they should take her home as they would undoubtedly want to do, wouldn't the killer follow? Three hundred miles was a short span for one who had brooded twenty years. Wakeley might refuse to let her go — but he was on the high road — where he might not see. . . .

Trembling, the nun sat down on Jinny's bed and clasped her hands tightly in her lap. Dear Lord, she prayed, don't let this poor child see how panicky and confused I am! Send us a solution . . . anything . . . anything to end this deathly suspense!

"Ted called up," she said. Her voice didn't sound too bad. "He asked for me when they told him you were asleep."

"Was I?"

"You had a nice long nap."

"Is he coming over?"

"After dinner this evening, yes. He said the boats won't be going out, not in the rain."

Ted had said a good deal more, too — that things were so disorganized at Waddy's it was like an anthill stirred up, everybody going off on tangents. The old gentleman had been the heartbeat of the place and without him there was chaos. But if there was anything Ted could do for Liz, he'd be right over. No, nothing, the Sister had said. And that was so terribly true. Nothing to do — except preserve her from the killer. Jinny had tried to do that very thing. I can't go chasing around the water front, Sister Simon pondered, a nun can't do things like that. I can't draw him out of his lair. . . . But Lizette could. Why not concoct some scheme using her as bait?

The idea was so repugnant that the Sister got up quickly and walked around the bed. Lizette was not watching. She was staring down at the ruined pages of her notebook, so drawn and limp that she seemed to be as drained of life as Jinny. That she was in danger now seemed as certain as the rain beating on the window. The killer was bound to strike at her, and there was no knowing where or when. But *if the time could be chosen for him.* . . .

"Lizette," the Sister said abruptly, "Lizette, would you do something to bring about a climax to this terrible situation? It may sound to you as if it would be dangerous, but actually you'd be safer than you are right now because the police would be protecting you. . . . Would you do it, Lizette?"

Lizette's dark eyes did widen with apprehension, but she said evenly enough, "Sister, I'd do anything — and I do mean anything — to get even for Jinny. What is it?"

Sister Simon found she had to sit down again, for her knees were giving way.

"Let me explain a little, Lizette. We know quite a few things about this man, whoever he is. He's connected with the water front, we know that. Dannie was frightened there, you talked to the mind reader and immediately a prowler crawls in the convent window, the laundromat girl told you that Jinny headed toward the water front with the suitcase."

"And she'd have had to be taken to the Gorge by boat. It's the only way you can get there from town." Lizette's face went even whiter. "Sister, do you think she was dead when he . . . "

"Dear, let's not do that, let's stick to what we know. Bartholomew Lawrence, for instance."

"Don't you mean Willis? And I didn't get the gun!"

"It doesn't matter. I called Bartholomew, the brother, this morning. He said Willis was a quiet boy, always satisfied with his job and his home and his girl. He was going to be married. There was no reason why he should disappear. So the only answer is that he was *made* to disappear."

"Somebody made him run away?"

"No. He was murdered. It's Willis' bones, not Steve's that were found in the ravine. Liz, Steve is still alive!"

The girl sat motionless for a long minute. Then she closed the notebook and laid it on the desk beside her.

"So he's the one Dannie saw that night."

"I'm sure of it, Liz."

"But why was she so scared to death?"

"Because she knew he was a killer."

"You mean of Jim McArthur?"

"Yes, the hunting accident that was not an accident at all. Somehow Elizabeth knew what had happened, and so Steve sneaked back and killed her, too. Perhaps he didn't think of Dannie's being a menace to him, not at that time. And Henry Waddy might have been inaccessible for some reason. Steve couldn't linger around town, waiting. Elizabeth was the only one who would have done anything to avenge Jim, anyway. He must have felt safe with her out of the way. He even dared come back here now, perhaps disguised in some manner."

"And then Dannie blundered onto him. But how, Sister?"

"I don't know. He didn't quite succeed with Vince Barron, but it's obvious he has killed everyone else who he thought could identify him."

"Jinny, too!"

"Everyone."

"Except me."

"Except you. . . . " Sister Simon took a deep and painful breath. "And you can be the one to — to bring him out into the open."

"What would I do, Sister?"

"Make him strike again. At you. And the police would catch him."

Sister Simon was amazed at herself, really. When she took the veil she had put off her identity as a policeman's daughter. Mother Richard would never approve. St. Augustine might get a kick out of it, but not Mother.

The girl stood up. "I'm ready, Sister. You want me to go down on the water front — is that it?"

"That's it, Lizette."

"Now?"

Sister Simon looked past her to the window. The rain would have driven away the crowd from the water front.

"No, no," she said quickly, "when the rain stops. Tomorrow morning. I'll call Chief Wakeley and explain all about it."

"He'll never agree, Sister."

"Oh, yes, he will!"

But the nun wondered, as she hurried out into the hall, whether Wakeley would be so easy to convince. For the present she need not concern herself with a decision. Perhaps, before she would find it necessary to make that decision, Wakeley's high road might have led him to the solution.

She opened the outside door and was hit by a splash of rain. Why walk down the long alley, unprotected, when she could just as well keep dry by going through the hospital? She darted across to the basement door and let herself in. Perhaps because the little dark door of the morgue was the dominant feature here, this corner of the hospital always reminded her forcibly of Dannie's murder. The Sister glanced at her watch. She had a few minutes before prayers, time enough to look in again on Vince Barron. Scarcely a half hour had passed since she had seen him, but he could have regained consciousness in the meantime. With these cases of concussion, you never knew. The elevator was down. She stepped in and pressed the second-floor button.

The door of Vince Barron's room was open a few inches, and Sister Simon tapped lightly, then put her head in. The white-haired nurse, standing at the foot of the bed, nodded.

"He woke up a few minutes ago, but he's still groggy."

"Has he said anything?"

"Nothing coherent. I gathered that somebody bopped him when he was putting his car away last night. He could have been knocked out for a minute and then came to enough to make it into the house. Funny thing how a blow on the head can work that way, sometimes. One patient I had — here he comes again, Sister."

The nurse moved close on the farther side of the bed. Vince was stirring restlessly and muttering. Sister Simon bent over him and took his limp hand in both of hers. She was almost certain he had mumbled the name of Steve.

"You're awake, Mr. Barron," she said quietly. "Open your eyes . . . come on . . . that's right. What about Steve? Was it he that hit you?"

He tried to shake his head, and winced with pain.

"Don't do that!" the nurse said. "Talking won't hurt you. But don't move your head."

"Did you see him?" Sister Simon persisted.

"No . . . no . . . nobody . . . but Steve . . . Steve's the killer."

"Why? Can you tell me why, Mr. Barron?"

"Always was a brat, never worked. Jim worked for what he had, but Steve wouldn't. Took everything away from Jim. Wanted Elizabeth, killed Jim to get her . . . but she wouldn't . . . wouldn't . . . "

The man's eyes closed. Sister Simon shook his hand gently. "Why did he kill Dannie? *Dannie*, Mr. Barron?"

"She must have known him . . . and Henry . . . too. . . . "

"Is Steve in town?"

The small sound he made could have been "no," but it also could have been the sigh on which he slid back into unconsciousness.

Sister Simon straightened, frowning. It would be cruel, as well as impossible, to try to waken him.

"That's why I haven't called Wakeley yet," the nurse said.

"By the time he'd get here our man would be gone again. By the way, Sister, who's this Steve character anyway?"

"If only I knew!" Sister Simon murmured, and she left quickly. Vince Barron's confirmation, hazy though it might be, was the first definite proof that her theory was right. Now she must decide whether to send Lizette off as bait and perhaps catch the murderer red-handed, or not to send her and leave him free to kill again. . . .

The nun, hurrying as always, traversed the old corridors to the alley, ducked out into the rain, and a moment later was running up the steps of the Octagon House. She had stopped to stamp off the bits of leaves which clung to her shoes when the door opened and Sister Joe came out. She had been crying. Carefully held against her she carried a letter in an envelope that had obviously been handled a good deal.

"Read it," she said, and thrust the letter at Sister Simon. "I couldn't forget it, although I tried. Read it, Sister, and tell me what I should have done."

Puzzled, Sister Simon looked down at the envelope. It was addressed to Sister Mary Joseph, St. Matthew's Hospital. And it had been postmarked a week earlier in Beechwood Falls.

Chapter Fourteen

LIZETTE changed her dress quickly, dug into her shoe bag for an old pair of sandals, and tied a kerchief over her head. She started to pull on her raincoat, then folded it instead and laid it over her arm. Opening her door, she looked both ways down the hall. No one was in sight. As quickly as Jinny had run away in the orchid dress, Lizette fled to the door and out. Under the portico she put on the raincoat. Then, forgetting to button it, she ran with the coat ballooning out behind.

It was easy running down the hill. Traffic was heavy on the bridge, but not with pedestrians, and she flew across and up the long slant of Main Street. The mind reader's tent was closed and deserted, the roller rink booming with young people in out of the rain. There was business too in the curio shops along the street. But not down in the river park. Lizette glanced over it as she hurried along the high sidewalk. At the top of the stairs where Dannie had paused in indecision, where Jinny had stood feeling so safe and courageous, Lizette also stopped. The rain beat upon her face and streamed down like tears. She hugged the coat around her. Over at the docks the *Triton* and the *Nautilus* were moored, stripped of their pennants and with the chairs turned upside down. The ticket booth was closed. No more desolate place existed on the face of the earth than this small, soaked area beside the river. Go back home, Lizette decided, bank down this terrific urge to do something instantly for Jinny. Tomorrow morning would be time enough — only Wakeley would never give in. That was why she had felt it so necessary to rush away immediately. Sister Simon could be right about who would be next — Lizette herself. If he could see her here, alone, whoever he was, surely he would realize what a perfect chance . . .

But there was no use lingering. The place was empty. She turned, hugging the coat, her foot on the step above, when she saw that she was not quite alone. Down by the wall, sheltered a little by the overhang of the sidewalk, the mud sculptor was at work. Completely absorbed in the mound of mud under his hands, he was paying no attention to her. She could even hear him whistling softly.

For a long minute she watched him. He had been one of those present when Dannie had become so frightened. And Jinny had found him fascinating. Slowly Lizette sidled down the stairs.

The sculptor evidently didn't know she was there until he stepped back to view his work. Then he gave her a mocking lift of the eyebrow and went on with the tune he was whistling. Lizette had not been able to see what he was doing, before. Now it was revealed, the lovely head of a girl. No body, just the head. The eyes were closed but she was laughing, and her hair was fanned out as if she had just tossed it gaily. Around the face, unbelievably delicate when you remembered it was all mud, was a wreath of flowers.

"That's beautiful!" Lizette exclaimed.

He paused as if he hadn't heard distinctly.

"Beautiful," she repeated.

He lifted a shoulder. "If you like mud."

Tilting his head, he studied the figure. For all the interest he took in Lizette, she might as well not have been there. He stood in the rain until his black shirt clung wet to his big shoulders. Then he returned to his work, down on one knee.

Oddly disappointed, Lizette turned to the stairs. But on the third one up, exactly where Dannie had paused, she stopped. Something stirred in the back of her mind — something she had seen. . . . Whirling, she stared at the man bent so devotedly over his modeling.

"Pico!" She said it rather loudly.

He took his time, but he sat back on his heel, finally looking at her.

Her breath was short, but she had to get it out.

"Pico, why are you modeling Jinny's head?"

Sister Simon stared down at the letter in her hand.

"You want me to read it?" she asked.

Sister Joe nodded so vigorously that a tear halfway down her cheek slipped sideways.

"Yes, dear. And don't spare me if you feel I did wrong in trying to forget it. There are so many sins of omission as well as commission, and I — well, read it, dear."

Sister Simon let herself down on the edge of a rocker. Opening the envelope, she took out the letter. It had been written in haste, half the t's not crossed and the dots nowhere near over the i's. Its message was urgent.

"Dear Mother Joseph, I may be in the Narrows by the time you receive this. I haven't quite decided what to do. But I was there three weeks ago, as you will remember, and I *saw Steve.*"

Those words were underlined. The pen, from there on, had trembled as it wrote.

"I believe I'll go back to the river park and have another

look at him, and then if I'm sure, I'll go to the police. He murdered Elizabeth. That was why she brought Diane to me that
morning of the fire, she was afraid for her. She didn't tell me,
exactly. She said she had had a visitor the night before, and
she was expecting him again, and she wanted the baby out of
the way. I know now it must have been Steve. He may think
Elizabeth told me all about it, and that I have told Diane, so
the only way I can protect Diane is to see that he's charged
with murder. He has changed his appearance a great deal, but
I'm sure I'll know, this time. Love, and pray for me. Damian."

Sister Simon's hand fell to her lap. Here was the evidence
to give to Wakeley, the meeting point of the high road and
the low! Before her Sister Joe stood, weeping quietly, her hands
gnarled together in anxiety.

"Did it matter terribly, dear? Me trying to forget?"

Sister Simon had to shake her head. How could she say
that the chain might have been broken in time to save Mr.
Waddy and Jinny?

"It didn't make one bit of difference," she said with all the
confidence she could muster. "But it will help now. I'm going
to telephone the policeman right away."

She smiled, taking the old nun by the arm to lead her inside, and Sister Joe's relief was pathetic. The central lobby was
deserted. From up in the chapel came the needle-thin chanting
of the Sisters at prayers. Old Sister Joe, unable to hear it, was
not reminded of prayer time. She sat down on the stairs and
mopped her wrinkled cheeks with her handkerchief.

Sister Simon dialed the number she had come to know by
heart in the past few days. A young policeman answered and
summoned Wakeley. She read him the letter.

"That's good, Sister," he said as she ended, but without
the elation she had expected. "It ties up the loose bits. We've
got the guy under lock and key. I gave you a ring a while

ago but they couldn't locate you — yeah. All we need is his confession."

The nun was surprised at herself for feeling deflated. "What a relief!" Then with all the enthusiasm she could gather, she asked: "Who is it?"

"I don't suppose you know Lou, the woman from the shooting gallery? That's hardly your beat. Well, Lou is a man. He hasn't admitted a d——, a thing, but the fingerprints will sew it all up. We got his prints and a whole slew of others off bottles and stuff in the trailer, so as soon as we get the identification on them from Washington we'll round up his playmates, too. This was a toughie, Sister. It's a great feeling to have it licked. Tell Lizette she can sleep for a week now, nothing to worry about. She's safe."

"Indeed I'll tell her," Sister Simon promised. "Congratulations, Chief."

She laid down the telephone and nodded and smiled at Sister Joe. In a minute she would write it all out for her, every detail, and reassure her again. But right now she would call Lizette.

She dialed again. A girl answered. The Sister asked for Lizette.

"But if she's asleep, don't wake her," she added. "I have some very good news for her, but it can wait."

"Did they catch him, Sister?"

"Practically."

"Oh, boy, wait till I tell her!"

There was the clatter of the phone being laid down. The interval was rather long. As the minutes went by, Sister Simon grew impatient. Surely it wasn't too much to expect the girl — it had sounded like Tony — to come right back. She could imagine butterball Tony perched on Lizette's bed, chattering away. She was ready to hang up when a voice finally came.

"Sister? I'm sorry I took so long. I was hunting Liz, but she's not here."

"Not there? Tony, where did you look?"

"Well, in her room and the shower room, and Hazel is just in from the cafeteria and she wasn't over there. I can't imagine . . . just a minute, Sister." There was a murmur, then Tony again. "Sister, Jean says she saw her leave a while ago. She had a bandana and a raincoat. Maybe she went for a walk."

"Perhaps she did," the nun said. "Thank you, Tony."

She hung up. There was no reason why she should feel uneasy over Lizette going out alone for a walk. Uneasiness had become a habit in the past few days.

Sister Simon picked up the pencil. "Steve is in jail," she wrote on the pad, and handed it to Sister Joe. She must break her habit of uneasiness now. Lizette could go anywhere she liked in safety.

The old nun nodded. "That's the proper place for him, if he's going around killing people. But it's a shame he went so wrong because there was so much good in him. A perfect physical specimen, too, only a little hard of hearing. But he had real talent, Sister."

Sister Simon looked a question, and Sister Joe nodded again.

"Oh, real talent! You should have seen the pictures he was always drawing. And the little figures he used to make out of modeling clay or mud or anything." She smiled and added as if this were a confidential matter, "I always said he could have been a wonderful artist."

Pico watched the girl run up the stairs to Main Street. She hadn't waited for him to answer her question about someone named Jinny. He stood until she was gone, then turned slowly and looked down at the blanket where people threw their dimes, now a soggy heap in the rain; at the figure of the camp cook with its ears disintegrating in the wet, at the mother and baby, the dog and pups, finally at the lovely, laughing girl. The spade was thrown down beside that one. He stepped on the blade, jumping the handle up into his hand. Then, methodically but quickly, he dug into the face. He had gone deep before the spade struck metal. He worked the object carefully out. It was a knife, short bladed and stocky. Picking up a dirty rag, he wiped the knife, ran his thumb over the cutting edge, and dropped it into his pocket. He left the spade where it had fallen, hurdled his rope fence and leaped up the stairs two at a time. On the street he stopped, then strolled toward the shooting gallery. Up ahead, beyond the vacationers scattered outside the shops, he could see the flying figure of the girl. She was heading straight for Waddy's.

Susan Chapin was having a dull afternoon. She expected quiet days, working in a mortuary, but this one took the prize. Snodgrass had looked in a while ago and said well, they certainly needed the rain, and then gone mooching off somewhere, probably up to the casket room to move things around again. Young Lombard had decided to clean the garage. Ted had taken the hearse down to the gas station. Susan was used to being alone in the afternoons, but the funereal stillness today was too profound a reminder that down in the preparation room Mr. Waddy lay on one of his own slabs. She jerked open the long drawer of her desk and glanced into the pocket mirror she had set in there at the proper angle to give her a view of her face. It wasn't ten minutes since she had done a complete job of mascara, lipstick, and powder. She slammed shut the drawer and reached out to turn on the radio.

The doorbell rang.

"Well, hallelujah," she said aloud, and tripped down the stairs and across Mr. Waddy's fine gray carpet to the door. She was just opening the door when the phone rang. It could go on for a ring or two. . . .

"Good afternoon," she said with the detached friendliness Mr. Waddy had taught her. Never let a person's appearance impress you, lesson number one; we meet people in times of stress, you cannot judge their status, either moral, physical, or financial, so treat them all with consideration and politeness. It was a good thing Susan remembered the lesson because the girl on the doorstep certainly looked like a street waif blown in by the wind. Her bandana, dark blue, was not meant for rain and it had run in streaks around her collar. The coat itself dripped puddles. But with the right make-up she would have been pretty.

The phone rang for the third time.

"Will you please step in?" Susan invited. "I'll have to answer that, but I'll be with you in a minute."

The girl stammered something, but Susan didn't catch it. She had to get the call. Mr. Waddy was very strict about calls.

It was a man asking for Ted.

"He's not here right now. He took the hearse over for an oil change. If you'd like to leave a message. . . . "

There was a second's silence on the wire. "Never mind, I'll get him at the gas station. He'll have to go to Newport."

"On a call?"

"Yes," the voice said instantly.

"What name, please?"

"He's going to Newport," the man repeated roughly. Then the line went dead.

Susan hung up the telephone slowly. This was most irregular. Surely Mr. Waddy would never permit Ted to chase off with the hearse without knowing exactly the destination and the name of a responsible party. But Mr. Waddy was not here.

"I'd like to see Ted, please," the girl said from the doorway.

Susan jumped. She had forgotten about her.

"Oh, I'm sorry, but Ted is out."

"Out?"

She looked as if she might faint, and Susan went to her quickly. "Why don't you come in and wait for him?"

"When will he be back?"

"I couldn't say, now. This fellow that just called, he wants a pickup in Newport. He's going to reach Ted at the gas station, so . . . "

"Nobody lives in Newport! That's a ghost town!"

"Well, even if nobody lives there, I guess somebody died there because this man said so and he sounded like he wasn't going to take no for an answer."

The girl went dead white and she seemed to speak with stiff lips. "A gruff voice, would you say?"

"Gruff is right. Muscles in it, if you know what I mean. You're Lizette, aren't you? Ted talks about you all the time."

"He sent Ted to Newport! Oh, he couldn't . . . no. . . . "

There was more to it but Susan didn't hear, because Lizette was gone, running down the steps and out along the rubber runner so fast she appeared to dodge between the raindrops.

"It's the big station right down on the corner!" Susan called after her. But the girl didn't stop or wave or anything. So Susan went back inside and closed the door.

She didn't feel right, not doing anything about the telephone message. Ted had been with Mr. Waddy longer than she herself, he'd have better judgment; and she might be able to reach him, yet. She took down the telephone book and was trying to remember the name of the gas station when the door chime again laid an urgent note on the silence.

A nun, just as wet as the girl, stood on the welcome mat. She had been running, or at least walking so fast the exertion had taken every speck of breath. She laid her hand on her chest and did nothing but breathe for a moment.

"Good afternoon, Sister," Susan said. "Won't you come in?"

"Lizette Carter — is she here?"

"No, she just left. Didn't you meet her on the hill, Sister?"

"I didn't meet anyone. Where was she going?"

"To the gas station." Susan's heart was doing uneasy leaps. There had been so much hanky-panky lately, and all revolving somehow around the hospital and the mortuary. "She's hunting Ted. He's down at — Harry's, that's it! — gassing up the hearse."

"I don't see how I could have missed her," the nun said, looking back down the street.

"Well, the way she chased off, she could have been to the moon by the time you came along," Susan said. "Ted had a call to go to Newport, and I guess she thought she'd catch him. If you want to wait a minute, Sister, I'll call Harry at the station."

"No, she could be there and gone while . . . "

Without finishing the sentence, the nun rushed off in the same way Lizette had gone.

"The big one on the corner, Sister!" Susan called.

The nun waved her hand. Again Susan closed the door. Just for her own satisfaction, she'd like to know what all the fuss was about. Leafing through the telephone book, she found Harry's number.

"Harry?" a man's voice answered her question. "No, Harry's doin' a battery. Whatcha want? Waddy's hearse? Just a minute, I'll look. I ain't Harry, but I'll look."

"O.K.," said Susan. "Even if you ain't Harry, you look."

After a moment the voice came again. "No hearse."

"Did a man leave a call for him?"

"Who for?"

"The driver of the hearse!"

"No. . . . Harry, any call for the hearse? . . . No call."

"Oh. Well, is a girl there?"

"What make?"

"Don't be funny!"

"I ain't. What make's she drivin'?"

"She's walking. In a raincoat."

"She ain't here neither. I'd of seen her."

"I bet you would," said Susan. "If the hearse comes, tell him to get in touch with me. Will you? Right away."

"I'll tell Harry, I ain't Harry."

"I know. Thanks anyway."

"Pleasure was all mine, ma'am."

Susan hung up. All she could do now was wait. Ted or Lizette or perhaps even the Sister would show up eventually, trailing one another. She might as well stroll to the kitchenette and see if there was any coffee.

Lizette, going past the filling station, did not even pause because all of the stalls were empty and the attendant stood under the awning chewing a wad of gum. Newport. Ted had been called to Newport, where nobody either lived or died, because he had been with her at the water front that night, he could have seen whoever it was that had frightened Jinny. Or Lizette herself might have told him. That was how the killer would work it out. So Ted too would have to be eliminated. But if he knew the plot, if he could be put on his guard before it would be too late . . . he was so strong, like a Roman gladiator, he could wrestle with an assailant . . . unless he was taken by surprise. . . .

Lizette was sobbing to herself when she reached the top of the long stairs. Peering over, she saw that Pico was gone. She wasn't afraid of him, exactly. He had remembered Jinny's face and modeled it without knowing who she was . . . or he had known . . . but what difference did it make? He wasn't here. Running down, she could see a couple of rowboats tied up, not the one they had used this morning, which was painted bright red, but two old green ones. Blinded by rain and tears, she stumbled down to the dock. One boat was half filled with water. She fumbled loose the painter of the other and jumped in.

The current carried her swiftly along without much help from the oars. It was a good thing. She couldn't think, much less fight a river. Reach Ted, warn him, get to him in time. . . . The rain felt refreshing on her face. But in spite of the laborious tussle she had with the boat, keeping it away from the willow roots, she was shivering when the dock came in sight. Someone was standing on the dock.

"Ted!" she screamed.

But almost with the cry, she knew it wasn't Ted. It was a short, dumpy figure . . . Merlin, the mind reader. She wasn't afraid of him. He would help her find Ted. Exerting all her strength, she pulled in quickly to the dock.

Sister Simon didn't even try to keep to a swift walk as she started down the hill toward the filling station. She ran. Her wet white skirts flapped noisily and her coif was beginning to wither around her face. People gaped at her, what few there were on the street, and several, she thought, would have asked what was the matter, Sister, if she hadn't chased on by. Cutting across the wide ramp at the station, she came to a panting stop before the attendant who stood under the awning chewing a cud of gum.

"Lizette," she choked out. "A girl! Has she been here?"

"In a raincoat?"

"Yes!"

"No, ma'am."

"Then how did you know she had a raincoat?"

"Somebody just called. Said so."

He had a long face like a horse. His jaw began to swing again.

"Was it a man?"

"Girl. Snippy."

Sister Simon made herself take a long, steadying breath. "What about the — the vehicle from Waddy's? Has it been here?"

"No, ma'am."

The nun caught hold of her wet veil which was flapping in the wind. Looking up and down the desolate street, she wondered almost despairingly what to do. *Where* was Lizette?

"She sure was skinnin' along," the fellow remarked.

"Who was?"

"That girl. In the raincoat."

"I thought you said she wasn't here!"

"Wasn't. She went by. Like she was shot out of a gun."

"Which direction?"

He jerked his head toward the river.

"You're sure about this?"

"Certain sure, ma'am. Ain't long, neither."

Sister Simon lifted her wet skirts slightly and stepped off the small landing. Evidently Lizette had gone to the mortuary to find Ted. Not finding him, she had decided to visit the water front. Alone. On an afternoon when no one would be around. . . .

"You from the hospital, Sister?"

"Yes."

"Harry's out for coffee. You wanta wait fi'teen minutes or so, I'll drive you back."

"Thank you, I can't wait. Thank you just the same."

She hurried away. She was getting wetter and wetter. Her veil slapped her back, her shoes made a squishing, a very continuous squishing because she went so fast. She certainly was doing all the things a nun ought never to do — being out in public alone, making herself conspicuous by talking to strangers — actually, in a way, chasing a murderer! Because murder could be the terrible climax to Lizette's escapade. I have to stop him, Sister Simon told herself, if only she would be in the park, not on her way to Newport. . . .

Looking down on the river park, the nun saw that it was totally, desolately empty. One rowboat, an old green one half filled with water, bobbed drearily at the end of the dock. Over close to the wall the mud figures were shiny wet in the rain. A newly dug hole was filling with water.

So Lizette had not come here. Ted could be in the same danger I'm in, how plainly she could hear the girl saying that, insisting on it. And she believed that Ted had gone to Newport. She would follow him.

Sister Simon leaned for a moment of weakness against the boat company's solid railing. Newport was two miles away. She was here. She had no money with her to hire a taxi, nothing but her rosary. She had to do something about Lizette. Call the police? Tell Wakeley he had the wrong man in jail, that Steve would have made a fine artist? But that would take time, for she would have to convince Wakeley first that there was very real danger. And in the meantime Lizette would be alone in Newport, the ghost town where nobody lived.

Groping for the crucifix of the big rosary that hung at her side, Sister Simon climbed the stairs and walked aimlessly to the curb. She had never felt more inadequate in all her life. There was no rule, no precedent to cover the situation of a soggy nun stranded on a street curb while, two miles away, a murderer made away with a victim she had delivered, although unwittingly, into his hands.

Chapter Fifteen

Lizette clambered up on the dock. Merlin did not heed her. He stood stiffly, not even turning his head. He wore no shirt, and his bare shoulders looked chilly after the heat.

"I'm so glad you're here!" she gasped. "I have to find Ted. . . ."

She stopped. The reason for Merlin's stiffness stood a few paces off, at the land end of the dock. Pico. With a gun.

Pico laughed.

"You don't expect to find Ted here, do you?"

"He had a call. . . ."

He laughed again. He was handsome in a brutal way, standing there with the rain beating on him.

"But you told the girl at Waddy's — was that because you knew I'd come here?"

"Exactly, my dear. Your devotion to your boy friend touched me — don't move!"

The order was for Merlin, who had staggered slightly.

"I'm not quite ready to kill you yet, not either one of you. But I will be, soon."

"He means it," Merlin said, and licked his lips. "Don't move."

174

Lizette, holding herself immobile, saw the very inside of fear. It was a cave like the one Jinny had died in, built by the cruelly cold eyes of this man who called himself Pico.

"So you're Steve," she said. She was surprised that she could speak.

He seemed to be surprised, also, and his mocking smile held a hint of admiration.

"I'd like to keep you, my dear. I really would."

"Then why not do it?"

That didn't please him. "You don't need to think you can keep me talking until help arrives. There won't be any help, not until it's too late."

"He means it," Merlin said again.

"Keep still, you fat fool."

Lizette managed to meet the man's eyes levelly. She should be saying the Act of Contrition, preparing for the judgment that would soon be upon her; but all she could think of was the gun, so steady in Pico's big hands, and the river running quietly under the dock. From the highway over beyond the trees came the sound of traffic. But a scream would never penetrate so far.

"Everything I ever wanted, I never had," Pico said, watching her closely. "Jim had it. Everything. Even Elizabeth. I killed Jim to get Elizabeth."

"And then she wouldn't have you," Merlin said with soft derision. "So you killed her."

"Don't," Lizette begged, but it was no more than a whisper.

Pico's face darkened, swelling with rage. Leave him alone, the man's out of his mind, don't goad him into killing us, Lizette begged silently, every minute is a promise of delivery! But a change had come over the mind reader also. Cowed and fearful before, now he regarded Pico with contempt.

"A big man with a gun," he said, still softly, "a great big

man. Powerful. Holding a gun on somebody is even better than your cheap blackmailing schemes."

Pico swore the vilest oaths Lizette ever had heard, but the stream did not deflect Merlin.

"Do you think we'd have had anything to do with you, Lou and me, if you didn't have something on us?"

"A jailbird and an old army deserter!"

Merlin shrugged. "We are what we are. You put us to good use, covering up for you. But we were not counting on covering up murder. Even if Wakeley hadn't pulled Lou in, the jig was up. I was going to the police."

"Public-spirited citizen!"

"Tonight, as soon as I could hitch a ride into town, I was going to the police."

"You've been spared the trouble, Smith."

"Of course," Merlin said. "Lou will take over." The gun wavered, but only a fraction of an inch. The mind reader continued evenly, "You don't imagine Lou will stay on the hook himself and not squeal on you? Why should he keep quiet? The ties of friendship? And how do you expect to make a getaway?"

"I got away once. I can do it again. I'll go back to South America." Then his hands tightened on the gun, and he raised it slowly.

Sister Simon had no time to begin the rosary. She hadn't been at the curb long enough to collect her thoughts even for the familiar rote when the truck pulled up before her. The gum chewer from the filling station leaned across the seat and threw open the door.

"Ride you to the hospital, Sister?"

She hesitated just a second. "I'd like a ride."

"Pile in."

She was in, and the door closed, and the truck moving before she added, "But not to the hospital."

"No? Well, just so's it ain't too far. Wife's waitin' for me to get home."

"To Newport. Please."

He was turning the narrow corner on to the bridge and he very nearly met a bus head on.

"Ain't nobody in Newport. I better drop you off at the . . . "

"*Please* take me to Newport! I don't want you to stay. Just get me there, quick!"

But he began to wag his head, thinking it over in time to his gum chewing. "Well, now, I wouldn't feel right about that. Ain't nobody there."

Oh, but there is, she wanted to cry out, there's a girl and a murderer. And I don't want you blundering along with me, alarming him so he'll stab her, or choke her, or something!

"I'm to meet someone there," she said. "It's perfectly all right."

He mulled this over thoroughly.

"She wants to go shoppin'," he said finally. "And to the doctor."

"Your wife?"

"Yuh. I'm s'pose to baby-sit the kids."

"Then you just drop me and go straight home. I'm absolutely able to take care of myself."

"Well . . . she's expectin'."

"Then you can't possibly disappoint her. It's very bad for women in that condition to be disappointed. And I'm sure she needs to see the doctor. So you go straight out this road, just follow the river. . . . How many children do you have?"

"This'll be five."

She asked him all the names and ages, who they looked like, everything she could think of. Any fewer children would not have served to get them to Newport. By the time they reached the ruined basement that was the only remaining emblem of the turn into the town, Sister Simon had the man's mind completely off the rather odd errand he was performing. With only a remark or two about hating to leave her, and how would she get home, he let her out of the truck. Then, making a turn that barely skirted the ditches, he drove back toward the Narrows.

Sister Simon struck at once into the woods. She was deep into the underbrush before she began to wonder in earnest whether this might not be a half-wit theory. Why hadn't she called Wakeley and at least tried to explain what she was about to do? Only he would have stopped her, of course, and done the investigating himself, taking his time . . . if he had believed in her idea at all. But there was nothing to do now but go on, plowing through grass waist high with burrs nipping at her ankles and a little wood's thing or two scuttling away as she approached.

And so she came out, before long, on the straggling, muddy expanse that had been Main Street. She stood still, listening. Rain hit dismally on ruined roofs. A big patch of ragweed in the middle of the place ducked its homely leaves under the onslaught of raindrops. Slowly she started forward. Would she have to look into every shell of a house that might shelter the killer and his victim, becoming a perfect target for him as she poked hither and yon? Because now she knew exactly how reckless she had been to come here alone. He could kill Lizette and her, dump them into some caved-in basement, and not even the father of the five children would ever be able to find them. Where would she begin?

And then, standing there so quiet in the patch of ragweed, she heard a man's voice. It was coming from the direction of the river. It sounded conversational, not in the least menacing. No girl's voice. Perhaps he had already — but then who would he be talking to?

As silently as the smallest thing in the woods, the Sister started toward the voice. The willows hid the speaker. She passed one after another of the ramshackle buildings and still the man was hidden. And then, suddenly, she saw him a short distance ahead, standing on the shore.

It was the black-haired artist. His back was to her. Facing her on the dock were Lizette and the mind reader from the Nickelodeon Palace.

Sister Simon paused. The gun was pointed directly at the two. If she were to alarm the fellow, if he were to feel any inkling of another person's presence, he would certainly shoot. So here she must remain, listening to this man's confession of murder, waiting for him to get around to shooting the two facing him, unable to do a thing to stop him. Jinny hadn't left the suitcase as she had been told, he was explaining. She had hung around, talked to him, and so he had had to take her for a boat ride. . . .

Revolted and sickened, Sister Simon made a movement and her toe hit a rusty tin can. The sound was tiny enough but she saw a faint reaction, quickly checked, by Lizette. If the girl had heard, so had the man. Stone still, the nun waited. Why didn't he whirl and shoot at her?

A perfect physical specimen but hard of hearing, that was what Sister Joe had said! Through a long frozen minute the Sister hardly drew a breath. The fellow didn't turn.

So he hadn't heard the slight noise. And if he actually couldn't hear well, then it might be possible to rescue the two out on the dock! How, she had no idea. She only knew that somehow she must try to overcome this man who stood with his insolent back toward her. And she must do it at once.

Praying in high gear, as she would tell Wakeley later, the nun walked slowly forward until she was only a few feet away from Pico. Lizette and the mind reader were steadfastly keeping their eyes away from her; but the strain must be terrific, she must act quickly, rush him before he could turn. . . .

The skirt of her habit fluttering wildly, Sister Simon started at a dead run across the intervening space. Fortunately, Pico did not hear her; indeed he was unable to hear the swish of the river past the pilings or any other ordinary sounds. She rushed desperately toward him, both arms held straight out before her. The impact was stunning. The man, thrown violently off balance, flung out his hands futilely. On the slippery bank there was no foothold, and he plunged on down into the water. The gun flew into the air and landed at Sister Simon's feet.

"Sister!" Lizette screamed. "The gun!"

"I have it!"

The gun felt good in her hand. The weapon was well cared for, she saw at a glance, and fully loaded.

On the dock the mind reader stood watching with a somewhat whimsical smile as if he enjoyed the joke. Pico, swearing, regained his balance against the pilings and came wading in to shore, flushed with anger.

"Get up beside him," Sister Simon ordered, gesturing with the gun. "Step along!"

Pico, taking his time, gave her a derisive look. He would put up with this state of affairs just so long as it pleased him, his manner plainly said.

"Lizette, come here," the nun said.

As if she were in a daze, the girl obeyed.

"Are you all right, Liz?"

"Yes, 'Ster."

"They didn't harm you?"

"Oh, no!"

"Now you two," Sister Simon dipped the muzzle at the men, "walk backward to the far end of the dock."

Pico shrugged, but they both did as they were told. The Sister advanced until she stood on the last rim of shore.

"That's far enough. Now stay there. If you move, either one, I'll shoot the two of you."

"You will?" Pico jeered. "Well, well!"

Keep calm, the nun cautioned herself, don't let him rile you. Show him that you mean what you say.

"If you don't think I can use this weapon . . ." She shifted the muzzle toward an empty bottle floating toward the dock and fired. The bottle shattered and disappeared.

There was a startled silence. Sister Simon needed that small interval to recover her own senses. Slowly the men turned to her, respect in the careful way they moved as if they expected her to blast off again if they didn't please her. The mind reader was pale under his stubble.

"Lizette," the nun said briskly, "go out to the highway and flag down a car. Ask them to summon the police. Then come back here. Run along, fast."

The girl went without a word. Sister Simon was trembling inside, but the tremors were not disturbing the confidence in her aim. If the artist took a step toward her, made any movement whatsoever — and he was angry enough to do it — she would indeed shoot him without the slightest hesitation. The other man, too. But she was not afraid of him, somehow.

The trembling left her. The pounding of her pulse died away in her ears. Now the only sound was the soft lapping of the water around the old dock.

I'm dreaming, Lizette thought as she ran along the weedy old Main Street, I didn't leave Sister Simon down there with two desperate characters, I didn't face death a few minutes ago.

But her errand was very real in her mind. Get out to the highway, stop a car, ask them to call the police and Ted . . .

"Ted!" she cried.

Of course she was dreaming! He couldn't have come so soon! But there he was, leaping through the underbrush like a frantic Tarzan, saying her name as if he couldn't believe his eyes. He caught her in his arms, squeezing her so hard she couldn't breathe, holding her away to look at her and catching her tight again.

"Liz, Liz, you crazy kid! What the devil brought you out here?" But he gave her no time to answer. Answers were unimportant, anyway. The marvelous thing was that he was here, and that out on the highway a police siren wailed to a stop and it was easy to imagine Wakeley jumping out of the car and crashing like Ted through the undergrowth.

"How did you know where to come?" Lizette asked, clinging to Ted.

"Susan. She said you were following me to Newport. And something about a nun."

"Sister Simon. She's down on the dock."

"What's she doing there?"

Lizette took his hand, turned, and began to run although there was no real need for haste now, not with the police catching up and Ted sprinting along without asking questions.

They came around the last of the willows, and stopped. Even to Lizette, who had been a terrified part of it so short a time before, the scene was hardly to be believed. A white-garbed nun, very wet but seemingly very much at ease, stood holding a gun on two stalwart men who stood obediently at the very edge of the dock over the swift running river.

"Well, I'll be darned," Ted said softly.

Wakeley, pounding up, stopped beside the two.

"What would you give for a picture of that?" he asked.

"Not a penny," said Lizette. "I want to forget it."

Drawing his gun, Wakeley strode forward. Lizette, leaning against Ted, closed her eyes. For this was the end, there was no more to see. And she was suddenly very, very tired and too near to tears.

Date Due

JUL 6	JA 06 '98		
JUL 29	DE 19 98		
AUG 3			
JAN 4			
JAN 17			
APR 10			
JAN 10			
JAN 21			
FEB 5			
MAR 19			
JUL 30			
FEB 20			
APR 26			
JAN 8			
SEP 5			
AP 30 '84			